A … ED DEATH

A BROCK & POOLE MYSTERY

A.G. BARNETT

ODDMOOR PRESS

MAILING LIST

For news on upcoming books and special offers, visit agbarnett.com

CHAPTER ONE

Ronald Smith hopped from one foot to the other nervously, his small frame a bundle of excited energy. Today was the day he was going to hit the big time.

As he was standing in the wings he could almost feel the excitement in the air, as though an electric current was zigzagging its way around the theatre and giving every person inside it a jolt of adrenaline.

He'd been working on the hit TV show *Foul Murder* for three years now, but his role as the pathologist consultant hadn't brought him the notoriety he craved. In fact, his colleagues openly mocked his involvement. This was what had spurred him on to request a walk-on part at least six times, all of which had been declined.

Then he had had his big idea.

There would be no more scoffing once they realised he was behind the greatest publicity the show had ever had.

His beady eyes scoured the audience that filled the small theatre. Various representatives from the national press's entertainment sections filled the first row. They quaffed their free champagne and laughed loudly as they swapped stories about whoever the latest celebrity to have an affair was. Part of the deal for tonight was that it was strictly a no-camera, no-recording deal. This was a live spectacle and wasn't going to turn into some YouTube video. The entire audience had been searched and their devices removed upon entry. If anything, it had added to the buzz and excitement in the place.

The crowd hushed as a low bass tone rose from the huge speakers that hung discreetly from the walls. Ronald Smith basked in the glow of it all. This was it. This was his moment.

POOLE WALKED behind Brock in a state of confusion. He knew that the inspector despised Ronald Smith. Though, to be fair to the big man, he hadn't yet met anyone who didn't despise Ronald Smith. The pathologist was a weasel, and that was giving a bad name to weasels. So why, then, had the inspector accepted this invitation to come to a launch event for the new series of *Foul Murder*? Whatever the reason, Poole was glad. He secretly enjoyed *Foul Murder* but would never pass this fact on to Brock, who would no doubt see it as a betrayal, and especially not to Ronald Smith, who would gloat like the toad he was.

He had been surprised when he had heard that the series six opener was being filmed in his new home county of Addervale, and even more surprised when he had heard that they were going to stage a press event announcing the return of the show in his new home town of Bexford.

Ronald Smith, of course, had been bragging relentlessly ever since the announcement had been made, casually mentioning where he planned to take the stars to dinner when they arrived, saying it had been his influence that had persuaded the producer to film the opening of the new series in Addervale.

Of everyone in the station, it had been Inspector Brock that Ronald had decided to invite. Poole could only guess that the intention was to rub his nose in Ronald's proximity to fame. Brock had insisted on his wife Laura having a ticket as well, but when Ronald had obliged, Laura had been caught up with work and so Poole had been invited in her place.

The truth was, Poole was in a bad mood. He had had a run in with Detective Sergeant Anderson earlier that day and, as always, he had gotten under his skin.

Anderson had been boasting about being assigned to a murder case, apparently over Brock and Poole. He had also bragged about how close the relationship between his superior, Inspector Sharp, and Chief Inspector Tannock was.

"Sir?" Poole asked as they passed through Bedford's main town square, the lights shining off the cobbles that covered its centre. "What's the deal with Chief Inspector Tannock?"

Brock looked curiously sideways at him. "What do you mean?"

"I mean, I've barely ever even seen the man. He doesn't ever seem to be in the office."

Brock sighed and pulled a battered bag of boiled sweets from his jacket pocket and offered the bag to Poole, who shook his head.

"Have you ever seen those old war films where the generals sit on top of the hill drinking tea while the men are down at the bottom, running into the gunfire and generally having a terrible time of it?" Brock said, popping a sweet into his mouth before returning the packet.

"Yes?" Poole answered, confused.

"Chief Inspector Tannock is one of those generals on the hill, and we're all down at the bottom getting shot at."

"Oh, right sir."

"But not for long," Brock added. "He's retiring soon. It's going to be a shock to old Sharp, I can tell you."

"Why's that, sir?"

"Well, him and Tannock go way back—old army buddies. I think they're what people refer to as 'part of the old boys' club', and when someone new comes in I think Sharp is in for a rude awakening."

"Right. Thanks, sir," Poole said, smiling. He was suddenly feeling much better about things.

They entered a side street, and after a few hundred metres, the New Theatre loomed. Its golden-coloured stone shone in the spotlights that surrounded it.

"Here we are then, Poole," Brock said, pushing at the large door and stepping inside.

The foyer was empty. They quickly crossed it, heading towards a bored-looking teenage girl who was standing behind a podium.

"You're late," she said, sighing as Brock handed her the tickets. "But they haven't started yet."

The inspector grunted and marched on through the double doors, which opened with a soft swoosh.

The lights were darkening as they stepped through into the theatre and music was beginning to pulse around the now hushed space. They took two seats in the last row, the only area where seats were still available, and settled down to watch.

The screen at the back of the stage lit up with the intro sequence to the show. The theme music kicked in, causing the crowd to whoop and cheer.

"Bloody hell," Brock muttered.

Poole turned to him, expecting to see the usual gruff expression, but instead, something else played across his expressive face. Poole was sure he was mistaken, but it looked as though there was a flicker of enjoyment there.

A man bounced onto the stage followed by a group of four people who all waved as the crowd applauded and whooped at an even greater volume. The man leading the group wore a bright blue suit with a crisp white shirt, its oversized collar jutting up, framing his stubble jaw.

Poole recognised him instantly as Jarvis Alvarado, star of the show and heartthrob of the nation. The rest of the number he recognised as fellow cast members. They took up positions on metal stools that had been whisked onto the stage by scurrying black-clothed figures.

Alvarado was standing in front of them, a microphone in his hand.

"Ladies and gentlemen!" he said, arms wide, his voice reverberating through the large speakers that hung from the walls.

"It is so good to see you all here tonight," he continued, "for what I'm sure is going to be the beginning of something very special!"

The crowd applauded as he flashed a set of bright white and perfect teeth that seemed to glow against his olive skin. The theme tune was still blaring from the speakers, its deep bass and heavy guitars sounding more appropriate for Wembley Stadium than the New Theatre at Bexford.

"And for you lovely people here tonight," he continued, "we have something very special indeed!"

He moved to the side of the stage and gestured to the heavens, both arms stretched out before him. There was a movement from above the stage and the crowd gasped as an exact replica of the office the *Foul Murder* team used on the show was lowered towards the stage floor behind the arranged cast.

Jarvis waved his arms to indicate he wanted more cheers from the crowd, and they responded with enthusiasm.

"Tonight, we will perform the opening scene from the first episode live just for you!"

The crowd cheered again, but the sound changed to a shocked intake of breath as the lights blinked out across the entire theatre.

"Sir?" Poole said, turning to his left and not seeing Brock, though he knew he must only be inches from him.

Brock's familiar gruff voice came back from the black. "Don't worry, Poole, I've got a feeling this is all part of the act."

Poole listened to the excited chatter of the crowd and tried to get his eyes to adjust, but it was no use. The place was built to not let natural light in.

"It could just be a power cut, sir," Poole continued. "Maybe an electrical problem?"

"Just wait, Poole," Brock's voice came back. "Never believe anything with these showbiz types."

Poole smiled in the dark. There didn't seem to be many people that Brock trusted. He had an in-built instinct that everyone was trying to pull the wool over his eyes.

The lights burst on with a brightness that made everyone in the audience blink furiously.

A piercing scream cut through the murmuring from the stage. A woman from the cast had risen from her stool and was pointing at the prone figure of Jarvis Alvarado, who lay sprawled at the front of the stage with a pool of blood spreading in a halo around his head.

Poole jumped to his feet. There were more screams now, they broke out all around as people pointed as people rushed onto the stage.

"Sit down, Poole," Brock said, folding his arms. "This is all part of it."

"Are you sure, sir?" Poole said, his eyes locked on the pool of blood.

"Of course it is! I mean, come on. The lights go out and then a murder occurs in those few minutes? It's like something for some terrible murder mystery rubbish on TV, which is exactly what this is!"

Poole took his seat again uncertainly as panicked figures shouted for help on stage.

"And here he comes," Brock said. Poole followed his finger to the right of the stage, where the small ferrety figure of Ronald Smith was scurrying towards the small gathering of people. "No wonder he invited us here," Brock said with a derisive snort. "The little git's got his own walk-on part."

They watched as Ronald Smith bent over Jarvis Alvarado. Poole noticed for the first time that the crowd that had gathered on stage were standing in a perfect semi-circle, allowing the audience to see exactly what was going on. He smiled to himself again. The inspector was right: this was all part of the show. They hadn't even dropped the curtain to hide the scene for the audience or made an announcement. This was all part of the drama. He leaned back, deciding to enjoy it all.

They watched as Ronald Smith fussed over the prone figure, theatrically taking his pulse and then looking into his eyes with a small torch. Then he paused and got to his feet, staggering slightly. He turned wildly around at the people on stage, who were now all staring at him. He looked out into the audience and shielded his eyes from the lights and he shouted in his squeak of a voice.

"Brock!"

The inspector jumped up next to Poole and began pulling him up and pushing him into the aisle.

"You're not going down there, are you?!" Poole said, surprised at the sudden change of heart.

"Yes, I bloody am," Brock answered, bustling them both down the aisle. "Because I know Ronald Smith, and I know there's no way on earth he's that good an actor."

CHAPTER TWO

Poole entered the lobby and pulled his ID from his pocket.

"I want you to close the doors. Nobody goes in or out until uniform arrive, OK?" he said to the bored teenager who was leaning on her desk, looking at her phone.

"I can't do that! You'll have to ask Mr Johnson." She pointed a ringed finger at a man who was now striding across the bright blue carpet towards them. He was a short, squat and sweaty man with a bald head that shone under the fluorescent lights.

"Can I help you?" he said, stopping as Poole stepped across his path with an apologetic hand raised.

"I'm sorry, sir, but there's been a serious incident and I need all the entrances and exits closed. No one in and no one out." Poole repeated, flashing his warrant card again.

The man blinked at him for a moment.

"But I can't do that," the man said, his brow creasing and causing a drop of sweat to gather and fall.

"I'm afraid you're going to have to or I'll have to arrest you for obstruction," Poole said. He watched the man's face twist as he took this information in, before he turned and began ordering staff to close the entrances.

Poole turned away feeling a strange mixture of being pleased and slightly disgusted with himself at the same time. He was happy he had forced the man to agree, but he hadn't done it in his usual manner. Poole considered himself a polite and gentle person in general, preferring to take the approach of working things out with another person rather than bullying them into submission. He realised with a slight jolt that his manner had been a lot like Brock's.

Poole moved back into the theatre and saw the imposing figure of the inspector on stage talking to an animated man in a black polo shirt.

Inspector Sam Brock was huge. Not fat, but tall and thick-limbed. If someone had set out to create the perfect rugby player, Frankenstein-style, then it would have looked a lot like him. Poole could tell by his body language that he was angry even before he'd reached the stage. Brock rose, looking down at the man that was waving his arms theatrically about him, arms folded. That kind of stillness from Brock was generally a sign that the other person should stop talking. This man didn't seem to be getting the message.

"It's just totally unacceptable!" the man was saying as Poole climbed up the steps to the right of the stage. He looked to his left, intensely aware that there were now roughly five hundred pairs of eyes fixed on him from the audience.

They were quiet now, as though there had been a brief intermission, but now the show had started properly. The only sound or movement came from the front press row who were frantically scribbling on notepads and cursing the lack of their phones.

"Poole," Brock said, turning to him. "When uniform get here, start them double-checking everyone in the audience for a recording device. They've been searched on the way in apparently, but someone must have got something in."

"Yes, sir," Poole answered.

"Right, Mr Hart," Brock said, turning back to the man who was staring back at him with nostrils flared. "Are you going to stop wailing and listen to me? Or do I need my sergeant here to arrest you and take you to the station?"

The man opened his mouth to retort, then paused and closed it again.

"Good," Brock said, taking a step forwards. "Then get someone to drop the bloody curtain right now," he growled.

The man turned and strode off to the wings, his beaky nose held high defiantly.

"Mike Hart," Brock said to Poole, staring after the departing figure. He turned around, his eyes sweeping the stage. "I've already made an announcement that nobody leaves. Uniform should be here any minute. I want them to go through the audience row by row. Get their name, address, contact details and statement, then let them go."

"Yes, sir," Poole replied, looking out at the audience. "It's going to take a while."

"It is, but right now I'm more concerned with what I'm seeing up here," the inspector said, his grey eyes still surveying the area in front of them. "Ron!" he barked suddenly.

Poole realised that Ronald Smith was standing at the back of the stage, his small head pale and downcast. He looked up sharply and trudged over as though walking to the gallows.

"And what about the actors, sir?" Poole asked,

staring at the four people who were gathered on the far side of the stage, drinking coffee from paper cups. Poole stared at the group, amazed by their calm attitude. Their demeanour seemed more in line with receiving a parking ticket than a colleague being murdered.

"I've told everyone who was on stage that they need to stay there for now, which is why I want the curtain down. They're not happy about it, and that jumped-up idiot Mike Hart was trying to get me to let them go back to their hotel."

"Sam," Ronald Smith said. His small ferrety face stared up at Brock as though pleading with him to save him from this mess.

"So, Ron," Brock said, his mood brightening at his discomfort. "A right little mess we've got here, isn't it?"

"Yes," Ronald said, staring down at his feet. "I just don't know how it could have happened!"

"Well, from where I was sitting it looked like the whole lot of you had planned for Jarvis Alvarado to be murdered tonight."

Ronald's round head jerked upwards. "You knew it wasn't real?" he said, his small eyes wide.

"Of course I bloody did. What I didn't know was that you were actually going to let the bloke get killed."

"I don't understand how it happened!" Ronald said again, wringing his hands as he glanced back to the body.

A movement made them turn back out to the audience where uniformed officers were now moving down the aisles.

"Go and give them their instructions, Poole. I'm going to see what's taking so long with this bloody curtain, and then we're going to go through what happened here before we start properly talking to people."

"Yes, sir," Poole said, hopping down from the edge of the stage.

The first officer he met was Constable Sanita Sanders. Her slightly lopsided smile flashed at him. "What trouble have you and the inspector caused now?" she said, putting her hands on her hips.

Poole put his hands up in mock protest. "Nothing to do with us, we were just in the audience."

She was a good foot shorter than Poole's six feet two inches, and her frame was slight with it. Her brown eyes flashed at him. "So, what's the situation?"

He filled her in on the details, slightly disappointed that the conversation had turned professional so quickly.

"Right." She nodded curtly, turning away and

getting to her task as he made his way back to the stage. Poole realised as he did so that the curtain had finally come down, and so lifted its heavy edging to duck under it.

The scene on the stage was pretty much as he had left it, apart from the white-suited figure of Sheila Hopkins from crime scene who was talking to the inspector next to the body.

He headed towards them, but his path was blocked by Ronald Smith.

"Poole," he said, his eyes darting left and right. "I hope I can trust you to be honest in this investigation?"

Poole frowned at him. "What's that supposed to mean?"

Ronald edged closer, his voice low. "Everyone knows Sam and I don't see eye to eye. If he's in charge of this investigation, I want to make sure he doesn't find some way of pinning it on me."

Poole's frown turned into a smile before he burst out laughing. Stopping short when he realised that others on the stage were looking at him, he wiped the smile from his face quickly as he caught Brock's eye. It really wasn't OK to be laughing at a murder scene. He turned back to Ronald.

"You have to be kidding?" he said. "If you knew the inspector at all, you'd know he'd never do anything that wasn't above board. Anyway, why do you think you've got any reason to worry?"

Ronald blinked and then turned and walked away.

Poole walked over to Sheila and the inspector and stared down at the body with them.

"Hit over the head, no murder weapon in sight," Brock said to him. "What was Ron's big joke?"

"He was worried you were going to frame him for the murder I think," Poole answered.

"Was he now?" Brock said, grinning. "Well I think we'll start with everyone getting to their positions when the lights went out, but then I think Ron should be our first little chat."

"How did Sheila get here so quickly?" Poole asked, watching her move towards the body.

"She was doing some open day at Bexford School down the road." Brock smiled. "She was already suited and booted and so came straight here." He turned and looked at Mike Hart and the small group of actors he was standing with. "What do you make of that, Poole?" he said quietly.

Poole looked up at the group and frowned. All of them were looking at their phones, looking more bored than upset.

"They don't look very cut up about it, sir," Poole said.

"No they don't," Brock replied before calling Mike Hart over.

"Inspector," he said when he reached them. "This really is too much. You can't expect us all to just stand around here with a colleague dead in front of us all evening!"

"Funny that," Brock said eyeballing him. "I've noticed that no one seems overly upset at this man's death."

Hart opened his mouth, closed it, and then opened it again. "We are all, of course, very sad. It's been a great shock. Which is why everyone needs to get back to the hotel to grieve properly."

Brock shook his head, amazed at Hart's ability to wriggle a situation around to suit his own purpose.

"Once the pathologist has arrived and taken the body away, I want ten minutes, no more. Then we can see about people going back to their hotel," Brock said gruffly.

"Well isn't Ronald Smith the pathologist here? Can't he get to work now?" Hart asked, looking around for the man in question.

"Of course he bloody can't," Brock answered. "He was right here when it happened and he's part of this whole thing. This is a murder enquiry, Mr Hart—we take these things seriously."

Hart's face paled at Brock's booming voice as he nodded and turned away, heading back to the cast.

It was another twenty minutes before the replacement pathologist arrived.

"Todd Peel," he said, extending a hand to both Brock and Poole.

"Thanks for coming in at short notice," Poole said, deciding that the inspector wasn't going to offer these pleasantries and so he should.

"No problem," the man said, smiling as he glanced across at Ronald Smith, who was glaring at him from the other side of the stage. "I hear Ronald's got himself in a little spot of bother?"

"Mr Smith was just here when the incident occurred, that's all," Brock said. "Now if you could hurry up, we're in a rush here."

The man nodded, looking slightly hurt, and moved away to the body.

Poole glanced at Brock inquiringly.

"Oh, come on, Poole. Ron Smith is a bloody pain but he's still one of ours. I'll not have some outsider suggesting he's part of a murder."

Poole nodded, his eyes remaining fixed on the inspector for a moment.

He sometimes felt that the more time he spent with Sam Brock, the less he knew about him.

"Listen up, everyone," Brock bellowed, his large

frame turning slowly. "I want everyone to move to the positions they were in when the lights went out."

There was a low grumble from around the stage, but people then began shuffling to their places.

Most of them left the stage, moving into the shadows of the wings. The cast of *Foul Murder* moved forwards and took their places on the stools.

"Why didn't Jarvis Alvarado have a stool?" Brock said as Mike Hart, the producer, approached them.

"Jarvis was going to be the presenter. They were going to take questions from the audience and he would move the microphone round."

"And who knew about this little stunt beforehand?"

"Well the cast, obviously, and the crew I told just tonight. I didn't want anyone to panic or anything, but I couldn't risk them knowing beforehand and it getting out somehow. The whole thing relied on surprise."

"Well you definitely got that," Brock said, pulling the waistband of his trousers up. "And where were you standing exactly?"

"I was on a phone call out the back. I didn't know anything was wrong until one of the people working here came and told me."

Brock nodded. "If you weren't on the stage, you can get off for now."

The man looked as though he was going to protest for a moment. Instead, he swept his hair back with his hand and strode off with his nose in the air.

Brock turned his attention to the stars of the show.

"Here we go then, Poole," he muttered out of the side of his mouth. "Let's introduce ourselves, shall we?"

They moved across to stand next to where Sheila was bent over the stage, scraping the floor with a small blunt blade.

Brock glanced down at her but decided to let her continue uninterrupted.

"Good evening. I'm Inspector Brock and this is Sergeant Poole."

There was no answer from the four people in front of them, just a mixture of eye rolling, bright white smiles and examining nails in boredom.

"Can I ask if any of you got up from your stools once the lights had gone out?"

"Of course we bloody didn't," a young man with a quiff of brown, sleek hair said. "It was pitch black! We're hardly going to go stumbling around in the dark, are we?"

Brock turned to him and the corner of his mouth rose slightly.

"Mr Turnbull, isn't it?"

"Yeah," the man said with an annoyed tone.

"Well, how about this Mr Turnbull," Brock said, moving across to him. "I think that all four of you—" he pointed to the end of the row and spoke as his finger moved down the line "—Miss Glover there, Mr Patrick, Miss Lennon, and of course yourself—all knew exactly where Mr Alvarado would be standing when the lights went out, and you all knew he'd then be laying on the floor pretending to be dead."

He had their attention now. They all stared at him from their stools like a class waiting for the teacher.

"I would imagine it would only be a matter of seconds for one of you to jump up and..." He stopped suddenly, his eyes cast downward.

"Sheila, please can you remove Miss Lennon's right shoe immediately?"

They all turned to the slim brunette who was sitting on the middle-right of the four stools. She looked down at her feet and let out a yelp as she jumped from the stool to the ground.

"Don't move!" Brock shouted and she froze instantly.

Sheila moved quickly to her and bent down to look at the sparkling blue shoe whose tip had a dark red stain across it.

"I must have stepped in it!" The actress shrieked

as Sheila removed it carefully and held the end up to the light.

"I want all of their clothes bagged for evidence," Brock said to Poole next to him. "And can you make sure Sheila checks all the stools carefully for blood?"

"The stools, sir?" Poole said, still transfixed by the celebrities in front of him.

"Well, they look like they'd make a handy weapon in the dark to me," Brock said with a grunt.

He looked around until his eyes landed on Ronald Smith, who was talking to a young woman he hadn't spoken to yet.

"Ron?" he said as he approached.

Ronald turned to him, his small round head creased with worry.

"I don't want you leaving until I've spoken to you properly, OK?"

"Of course, Sam," he said, his hands wringing in front of him. "This is Jane Marx, by the way—she's the stage manager here at the theatre."

"Nice to meet you, Miss Marx. And where were you when the incident occurred?"

"I was in the wings, the opposite side to Ronald here. I was the one who turned off the lights, from a main switch over there."

"And did you notice anything unusual when the lights were out?"

"No." She shook her head. "I mean, I couldn't see a thing. When I turned them back on I stayed where I was. I thought everything was fine until I saw Ronald's reaction. Then I ran back to get Mr Hart, who was on the phone in the back corridor."

"OK, thank you. We'll need you to make a formal statement sometime tomorrow, but for now you can go home."

She nodded her thanks and Brock and Poole walked off to where the curtain hung at the front of the stage.

"I'm guessing the cast are staying at the Sinton next door?" Brock asked.

"Yes, sir."

"Then let's get them back there and we'll take a brief statement from each of them while it's fresh in their minds."

CHAPTER THREE

The Sinton Hotel was Bexford's most luxurious establishment. Its thick stone walls looming in an imposing fashion just off the main town square on a smaller side street. The lobby of the Sinton had tall but narrow windows and was dimly lit from Victorian lamps that hung from the walls.

"Why's it so bloody dark in here?" Brock muttered as they moved across the lobby.

"I think it's to set the mood, sir," Poole answered.

"And what sort of mood is that? One where you're bloody angry that you've stubbed your toe because you can't see where you're going?!"

They reached the front desk and the young man stationed there directed them towards the bar area where the cast of *Foul Murder* was apparently gathered.

"Inspector," Mike Hart said, rushing to meet them as soon as they had passed through the brightly glazed door which led through to the bar area. "I think it would be best if the interviews could be conducted here. We've made sure we have sole use of the room for this evening, anyway." He saw their questioning eyes. "For the after-show party. Naturally, that's not going to happen now."

Poole glanced across at the group in the corner and thought it looked like it was indeed happening. They were lounging on the deep-red sofas, drinking from tall flutes that contained something bubbly. Somebody had clearly said something funny as they all suddenly burst into laughter.

"I can see they're all still very upset," Brock said, his eyebrows raised. "We'll talk to them on the other side of the room. I want to speak with Isabella Lennon first." He turned and marched to the far side of the room and chose a table that was slightly obscured from the cast members by the edge of the dark mahogany bar.

"Something that's been bothering me, sir," Poole said as he took a seat next to him and pulled his black notebook from his jacket pocket.

"Yes, Poole?"

"Well, back at the theatre I noticed that you knew the names of all the cast members." He glanced to his right and saw a slight flicker in the inspector's expression before it landed back to its normal, inscrutable gruffness.

"Research, Poole. You should always do your research on a case."

Poole was about to point out that they hadn't known it was going to be a case until Jarvis Alvarado had been killed in front of them, but was distracted by the slender frame of Isabella Lennon moving towards them.

Brock rose as she arrived, catching Poole off guard. He clattered his pen down and got up just as both Isabella and Brock took their seats.

"So, Miss Lennon," Brock began, glancing with annoyance at Poole as he took his seat again. "Can you tell us exactly what happened tonight when the lights went out?"

She shook her head sadly, causing two ringlets of sleek brown hair to shift across her forehead. "Oh, it was terrible! Poor Jarvis." She pulled a small handkerchief from the pocket of her skinny jeans and dabbed at her eyes.

Poole felt Brock sigh next to him, clearly seeing it, as he did, as a performance by an actress.

Poole studied her for a moment. She was beautiful, but in a strange, alien way. Her face was rounded like a doll's, and her eyes were small and dark. Poole had always quite admired her on the show, but now she was up close she seemed overly thin and her eyes were hard and cold.

"The moment when the lights went out, Miss Lennon," Brock said. Poole could hear the patience wearing thin in his voice.

"Well," Isabella said, placing the handkerchief back in her pocket, the performance clearly over for now. "I was sitting on my stool; the lights went out. When they came back on, Jarvis was lying on the floor just where he was supposed to be. I didn't think anything had gone wrong at first."

"And you didn't get up from your stool at any time when the lights were out?"

"No."

"And did you hear anyone else move?"

"No, all I heard was Jarvis landing on the floor."

"Landing? What do you mean by that?"

"Well I guessed it was Jarvis messing about. He was like that—always messing about."

"What exactly did you hear?" Brock asked.

"I heard him throw himself on the floor!" she said, annoyed. "What difference does it make?"

Poole and Brock glanced at each other.

"You do realise Jarvis was murdered tonight?" Brock said, speaking slowly.

"Oh yes, just terrible," Isabella said, the

handkerchief reappearing and dabbing at her dry eyes as though she was on autopilot.

"And did you go near Jarvis once the lights had come up?" Brock continued.

"God no! Once I realised what was going on I got the hell away from it."

It, thought Poole.

"If you didn't go near Jarvis, then how did you step in the pool of blood around his head?"

She blinked her small, dark eyes. "I must have just walked in it as I got up from my stool."

"It was a good few feet away from your stool." Brock's voice was quiet and low.

"I..." She blinked again furiously. "I remember now. I did go over when that little man was looking at Jarvis and then I got away quick when I realised what had happened. Look, is this going to take much longer?"

"What was your relationship with Jarvis like?"

"Oh, he was all right. Quite funny," she said, shrugging.

"And do you know if he had any enemies at all?"

A smile flashed across her thin lips before she resumed her blank expression. "No. Everybody loved Jarvis. I can't imagine why anyone would want to kill him. Are you sure it wasn't an accident?"

"Unless he beat himself to death with the

microphone, I'd say so, yes," Brock answered in an annoyed tone. "OK, Miss Lennon, you can go now, but please remain in the hotel for the time being."

She gave a little sigh, got up and walked away.

"Bloody hell," Brock muttered.

"Bit of an odd one, sir," Poole said. "Interesting acting skills."

"Glad you noticed, Poole," Brock said, stretching his arms up above his head. "Go and fetch another one, will you?"

Poole got up and walked over to the table where Isabella had re-joined the others and was now sipping a cocktail.

"I'll go," a young man said, jumping up before Poole could say anything. "Best to get it over with, eh?" he said cheerily.

Poole nodded at him and walked back across the room.

"Eli Patrick," he said, extending a hand to Brock as he reached the table. Brock shook it with a grim expression.

Poole took a seat, wondering why the man hadn't offered to shake his hand or introduce himself to him. Clearly he wasn't of the required seniority.

"So, I guess you want to know what happened when the lights went out, right?" Eli said, leaning forwards and smiling.

His voice had a plummy, Oxbridge lilt that suggested he came from money, while his fresh face and enthusiastic manner showed his youth.

"That would be a start, Mr Patrick, yes," Brock said slowly.

"I'm afraid nothing happened at all! Well, apart from poor Jarvis kicking the bucket, obviously."

"You didn't get up from your stool?"

"Lord no. I'd have fallen over in next to no time. I'm a terrible klutz, you know." He threw his head back in a braying laugh.

"And did you hear any movement from anywhere else?"

"No, just heard Jarvis splat on the floor. Thought he was mucking about, but I guess not, eh?" He stared off into the distance, as though the realisation of what had happened had suddenly come to him.

"Were you close to Jarvis?" Brock asked, pulling Eli from his thoughts.

"Oh, not really," he said, sighing. "I've only been on the show for one series and he's the big star!" He emphasised this last part by placing his hands palm out and shaking them.

"And were people jealous of his fame?"

"Jealous?" Eli said, laughing. "Of course they were! Everyone! That doesn't mean anyone would want to bump him off, though, we were all just riding on his coattails. Him being so big helped everyone on the show."

"You can go back to your seat now, Mr Patrick. Can you send over another of your colleagues, please?"

"Course! Nice meeting you chaps. Hope you catch the bugger who did this to poor Jarvis."

"He seemed fairly happy," Poole said when he'd left.

"People with only a few brain cells often do," Brock said, sighing. "I don't like this, Poole. The lights went out, no one moved, no one heard anything?"

"With the noise from the audience, maybe it's not that surprising?"

"Yes, but if we end up with no one seeing anything and no one hearing anything, what are we left with? There seems to be no sign of a murder weapon yet." He sighed and leaned back in his seat.

The rangy figure of Jonny Turnbull arrived at their table, slumping into the chair opposite them like the school bully visiting the head teacher.

"Come on, then, let's get this over with so I can get out of this sinkhole," he said, spitting the words out with a snarl.

"You're not going anywhere for the moment; I

need you all to stay in the hotel," Brock said, his voice level.

"Ha!" Jonny said, shaking his head. "What is it; got some little deal with the hotel owner, have you? Is he your cousin or something? Thought you could keep us locked up here and bleed us dry? Well, the show's paying, so you'll have to take it up with Mike." He leaned forwards and narrowed his eyes. "But I go where I want."

"Not if you go to jail for the murder of Jarvis Alvarado," Brock said.

Jonny straightened up. "I don't know anything about Jarvis dying," he said quietly, his bravado shrinking visibly.

"What happened when the lights went out?"

"Nothing. The whole place was pitch black. I couldn't see a thing."

"And did you hear anything?"

Jonny turned, glancing over his shoulder towards the table where the others were sitting, partly obscured by the bar.

"I think someone got up," he said quietly. "A stool squeaked on the stage like someone had moved it."

"Anything else?" Brock asked.

"Well, I heard Jarvis hit the deck."

"And was that before or after you heard someone

get up?"

Jonny looked up, his brow furrowed. "After, I think. Look, I don't know. I wasn't really paying attention!"

"And afterwards?"

"Well everyone was sitting down when the lights went up, and I saw Jonny lying there with all the blood. But that's what we thought we'd see. He had a blood capsule and was supposed to crack it so it looked real. I didn't know he'd actually croaked until that little weird fella came on."

"Ronald Smith?"

"I don't know, that little freak who's always trying to hang around us. A doctor or something."

Poole noticed the flicker of a smile play on Brock's lips.

"That's all for now, Mr Turnbull. If you could send Miss Glover over."

Jonny huffed and stormed off as though he had just suffered some great injustice, no doubt for the benefit of those at the other table.

"So, someone moved when the lights were out?" Poole said.

"Maybe," Brock answered. "Or Jonny Turnbull is trying to deflect us from himself. But it might explain how Miss Lennon got that blood on her shoe. We won't know until we hear the pathologist's report."

He looked up as a woman with bright auburn hair and a sharp, intelligent face approached. She was standing in front of them, her arms folded over her red dress.

"Gina Glover," she said, her eyes sparkling as they ran up and down the inspector. "According to the others you're still saying we can't leave?"

"That's right," Brock answered. "Everyone involved in the show will have to stay here until we're able to take statements from everybody and establish their whereabouts when the lights went out."

"Well I don't see the need," she said, shifting the weight on her shapely hips. "It's pretty obvious who did it, isn't it? So I don't see the point in keeping us all here."

"And who would that be?" Brock asked.

"That little weaselly chap, Ronald or something. All of this was his idea and he hated Jarvis."

"Hated him? Why?"

"The same reason everyone else did." She shrugged. "Jarvis was an arrogant bully who thought he could treat people like crap. That little bald creature got more than his fair share. Jarvis liked to humiliate people like that publicly." Her voice quietened. "He got a kick out of it."

"Would you like to take a seat?" Poole asked, gesturing at the chair in front of her.

"I'd rather stand," she said flatly.

Poole nodded, though he was finding it slightly disconcerting.

"And you were on your stool when the lights went out?" Brock asked.

"Of course. Where else would I be?"

"And did you hear any movement from anyone?"

"I don't think so," she said, sighing. "I mean, I heard Jarvis throw himself to the floor and then the audience were making a bit of a racket. When the lights came on I jumped up with the rest of them looking shocked and all that business, but I saw something was wrong as soon as I looked at him." She took a deep breath as though steeling herself to say something. "His eyes were open. Then that little doctor came on and started panicking and I'm guessing you know the rest."

Brock nodded. "And what was your relationship with Mr Alvarado like?"

She began to bite her bottom lip gently as she leaned on the back of the chair.

"I thought we were close once—we knew each other from back when we were starting out—but I don't think anyone really got close to Jarvis. I'm not sure anyone even really knew him at all. He ticked off almost everyone he ever met, though, so I doubt you'll be short of suspects."

"Except there were only the four of you on stage at the time of death," Brock said purposefully.

She frowned at him. "Are we done?"

"For now. Can you send over Mr Hart please?"

She turned and walked away.

"Eyes down, Poole," Brock muttered. Poole wrenched his gaze away from the rear of Gina Glover and looked back to his notebook, cheeks reddening.

"So, which one do you fancy?" Brock said. Poole looked up at him with a look of panic. "For the murder I mean, Poole," Brock said. "For goodness sake." He shook his large head.

"Sorry, sir," Poole answered, glancing back towards the other side of the room. "I'm not sure. I mean, it must have been one of them, mustn't it?"

"Not necessarily," Brock said. "Maybe someone from the stage jumped up and did it, maybe someone ran on from the wings. The whole place was pitch black."

"But how would anyone have been able to see to do that?"

"Maybe they eat a lot of carrots." Brock grinned.

"Are we all done for the evening?" Mike Hart said, approaching their table.

"Almost, Mr Hart," Brock said, smiling. "Can I ask where you were when the lights went out?"

"I was on the phone," he said irritably.

"I asked where you were, Mr Hart, not what you were doing."

"I was in the corridor, backstage."

"And can anyone verify that?"

"The person I was on the phone with, I guess. Steve Hatten from the station. They were checking up on the launch."

"I bet they're not too happy now," Brock said, shifting his weight in his seat. He glanced at his watch. Half nine. If he was going to be working this late, he needed to be doing it with a beer.

"That'll do for now, Mr Hart. We'll want to talk to you more, but not tonight."

"Right, I'll go and let the others know, then."

"No one can leave, though," Brock said sharply. "I want everyone here tomorrow morning."

Mike Hart nodded miserably and turned away, heading across the room.

"Do you want a lift home?" Poole said, closing his notebook.

"We're not going home yet, Poole."

"No?"

"No. I think it's time we took our colleague Ron for a drink, don't you?"

Poole smiled. "Sounds like a plan, sir."

CHAPTER FOUR

As they settled down in The Mop & Bucket, three pints of Bexford Gold in front of them, a silence fell across the table.

In fact, thought Poole, for someone usually so full of things to say, most of them annoying, Ronald Smith had been remarkably quiet on the walk across to the pub. They had found him back at the theatre, still hovering around the crime scene, watching the goings-on with a sad air, unable to help but unable to leave.

"So," Brock said. "Do you want to tell me how this all came about?"

Ronald sighed and turned his pint glass slowly in his hand.

"A few months ago I heard that they were

thinking of doing some big launch event for the new series. I suggested they should do it here."

"Why?"

"The first episode is set in a country house in Addervale. I suggested they should make it a local event and..." He paused and looked up at them nervously before returning his gaze to his drink.

"And what?" Brock prompted.

"Well, I had an idea how they could really get a lot of publicity."

"To fake Jarvis Alvarado's murder?" Poole said.

"Yes. And I thought doing it here, it would be easier to set up and make sure no one knew what was really going on. In London the press would have been all over it."

"And you didn't think it would be a good idea to tell us about this?" Brock said, his voice like steel.

"I didn't see the need!" Ronald squeaked. "It was all safe, just a big joke, really!"

"Well somehow I don't think Jarvis Alvarado's family are going to see it like that," Brock said.

Ronald's head drooped. "I don't understand how it could have happened."

"Tell us what was supposed to happen," Poole said as Brock took a huge swig of his pint.

"Well, when Jane made the lights go out, he was supposed to just drop to the floor and break the blood capsule. Went the lights came back on we thought everything was normal, but when I got to him..."

"You realised the blood was real?" Poole finished for him.

Ronald nodded miserably. "I only had a quick look, but it was obvious he'd taken a serious blow to the head."

"We searched everyone on the stage. None of them had a weapon," Brock said.

"Then someone must have run on and done it," Ronald said. "But I was standing in the wings waiting to go on and I think I would have noticed someone moving past me."

"Did you have a light on in the wings?"

"No. We tried that in rehearsal, but when it's that dark everywhere else, you could see even a little pen torch. We decided to just turn everything off. As long as no one moved we thought it would be all right."

"Who was with you in the wings?" Poole asked.

"There was just me on my side," Ronald said, frowning. "Mike had gone off to make a phone call and Jane was the other side, working the lights."

"And there was no one else there at all?"

"No. We made sure it was a skeleton crew because we didn't want the secret getting out. The only other person involved was Simon Keller, who was up in the lightbox, doing lights and sound."

"Why didn't he turn the lights off from up there?"

"Oh, he just controls the stage lighting. There's a main switch on the stage, like a safety thing which turns everything off, house lights as well."

Brock drained the last of his drink and placed it down heavily.

"You're a bloody fool, Ron," he said, fixing him with a hard stare. "But we're going to do what we can to find out who really did this and get you off the hook."

Ronald nodded in a jerky little motion. "Thank you, Sam."

"That is, of course, unless you did it."

Ronald's head jerked up, his small eyes wide. "Sam, you don't think I could have?"

Brock sighed and shook his head. "No. Despite you being a grade one prat, I don't think you murdered Alvarado, but a lot of people will. Think about it—this guy apparently wound you up a lot, made fun of you?"

Ronald nodded as though in a trance.

"Then you come up with this idea of faking his death with you in a prime position to run on and clobber him. I can see that a prosecution would point to your medical knowledge and suggest you'd know exactly where to hit someone to put them down for good."

Ronald was breathing heavily now, his perfectly round dome glistening in the dim lighting of the pub.

Despite it being only a Thursday night, the place was surprisingly busy. Ronald jerked his head around as though he was suddenly under the impression the entire pub was listening in and mentally tagging him as a murderer.

"It was someone tall," he blurted out as he turned back to them. "He was hit on the back of the head, but it was right at the top. Jarvis was about five foot ten, so it must have been someone pretty tall to hit him there."

"Or someone hit him when he was on the ground, pretending to be dead," Poole said. Ronald frowned at him before his shoulders sank again.

"Can you think of anyone who would want to kill him?" Brock asked.

"The man was a nightmare," Ronald said sulkily. "He was always trying to make other people feel small."

Poole resisted the urge to suggest that he wouldn't have had far to go with Ronald Smith; it wasn't the time.

"He just never, ever stopped, always digging

away at everyone. They only put up with him because he was the big star."

"Right," Brock said, stretching. "I think it's time we called it a night. Go home and get some rest, Ron. There's a long way to go in this yet, and whether you like it or not, you're right in the middle of it."

CHAPTER FIVE

"Hi, Mum," Poole said as he stepped through the front door of his flat. His mother was on the sofa, stretched out with some sort of face-mask on and cucumber slices on her eyes.

"Hi, love. Did you have a good day?"

"Oh, the usual—went to a show, someone got murdered."

"Oh, a whodunit, was it?"

"Something like that," he said as he reached into the fridge and grabbed a beer.

He noticed that he had been reaching for a beer more frequently since his mother decided to move in with him while she looked for a new place. Now he thought about it, he couldn't remember her ever actually asking him as such; she had just turned up with three large suitcases and announced she was moving to Bexford.

It was all because of his father. A month ago he had been released from prison, and his first port of call had been to track down his son. Brock had faced up to him and told Jack Poole to keep away, and so far, he had. But Guy knew that wouldn't be the end of it.

His father told him he was looking to move nearer to him, that he wanted to be part of his life.

So, while having his mother staying with him was a strain, to put it mildly, he also enjoyed knowing she was here, and safe.

"Any luck with looking at places today?" he said casually, trying not to sound as though he was hounding her out.

"No—Bexford is just so blooming expensive! I don't know how anyone can afford to live here!"

Guy thought that people could afford it because they had jobs, but restrained himself from saying so and instead turned to more practical matters.

"What do you fancy for dinner tonight?" he said, opening the fridge again. It was full of beer, plastic pouches of various gooey substances his mum applied to her face, and kale. Guy had questioned why anyone on earth would need so much kale at once, but his mother had explained that Ricardo told her that it was a superfood and would transform her, both in spirit and body.

After the violent incident which had resulted in her husband being sent to prison, Jenny had thrown herself into the spiritual world—which included throwing herself onto a man called Ricardo, who as far as Poole could tell was part salsa dancer, part yoga teacher, part guru and all conman. His mother seemed happy, though, and so he bit his tongue other than to make sure she was careful with her money.

"I've already eaten," her voice came from the sofa. "I tried that sushi place in town. Not bad, as it goes."

"Right," Poole said, closing the fridge slightly harder than necessary. He had noticed that his mum hadn't managed to contribute to the food, shopping or the cleaning yet. Bearing in mind that generally the only things on her calendar were yoga and the occasional aura cleansing (whatever that was), he felt she might have chipped in more.

He moved to the kitchen drawer he reserved for random odds and ends, and most importantly takeaway menus, when the sound of the letterbox opening made him pause. It was late for anyone to be dropping something through his letterbox, and only the postman had the key to enter the main door downstairs. Anything else was dumped in the communal box in the lobby and was picked up whenever people could remember to check it.

He turned and walked to the door where a small white envelope lay in front of it. He picked it up and turned it over. Just his first name, hand-written.

Something sent a shiver down the back of his spine, and he froze for a moment before his brain kicked in again and he wrenched open the door and burst into the corridor.

There was no one there, just the cold flat tiles and the cream-coloured walls. He listened, seeing if he could hear footsteps echoing from below, but there was nothing.

He ran down anyway, reaching the door and running out into the small car park at the front of the building.

There was no one in sight, no sound, no movement.

His heart pounding, he headed back up the stairs where he found his mum in the corridor, cucumber slice in each hand, her ghostly face looming in the dimly lit hallway.

"What on Earth's got into you?' she said, annoyed. "I thought something had happened to you!"

"We got a letter," he said, moving past her and back into the flat.

"A letter? There was nothing in the post this morning."

"This was just delivered. Look." He turned the envelope around and watched as his mother's face paled. He knew already what she was going to say, had known it from the moment he had seen the letter.

"That's your father's handwriting," she said, her voice barely a whisper.

He moved across to the small table and chairs that were against the left-hand wall of the kitchen area and took a seat. He waited until his mother had joined him and then opened the envelope carefully.

Guy,

I know how you feel about me but I'm not going away until we talk properly. Meet me on Friday night at the market wine bar, 10 pm.

I know what's done is done and that you might never want to look at me as your dad again, but there are things you need to know.

Dad.

POOLE LOOKED up at his mother.

"Well, you can't go," she said, her voice shaking. She stared at him, her brow furrowing as he didn't respond. "Guy, you know you can't."

"I need to," he answered, the dark tone of his voice surprising himself as well as her. "This is going to hang over me for the rest of my life unless I talk to him. I need to face this. I need to face him."

"It won't do any good!" she said, throwing her hands in the air. "Your dad lied to us. He ruined everything! That poor boy died!"

"I know that," Poole said quietly. "And that's why I need to talk to him. It's time."

His mother slumped back in her chair, shaking her head as though it was on fire.

"What does he mean, 'there are things I need to know'?" Poole said quietly.

Her gaze snapped back to his. "He's a liar, Guy. You know that."

"And what lie do you think he's going to tell me?"

She got up and walked across to the small wine rack and pulled a bottle of red out.

As he watched her pour a glass, he thought of how few conversations they had had about his dad, about what he had done. Despite the incident that had changed his life, making him determined to become a police officer, Guy had never read any newspaper articles on the case, he never asked to look at the case files.

The only information he really had about what had happened was from other kids at school—the ones who taunted him that his dad was a gangster, that his dad was a murderer.

He had fought back, become immune to it all, and gradually they moved on to another hot topic. He had tried to forget it all rather than face it. He buried it as deeply as he could while he threw himself into his career, becoming the youngest Detective Sergeant in the country.

Then his father had been released, and now it felt as if his past was always right behind him.

"What is it, Mum? What does he think I need to know?" he said again, as she took a seat.

"To tell you he's innocent, I'd imagine," his mum laughed, without a hint of humour.

"Innocent?" Guy said, staring at her.

"Oh, come on, Guy. The man is a born liar. All those late nights he worked, all the times he was away on business trips, what was he really doing?"

Guy studied her face. It was contorted with pain and anger—an anger she had hidden behind herbal remedies, yoga and crystals, and a pain that none of those things had healed.

"Did he tell you he was innocent?" Guy repeated.

"Yes! Despite the fact they found goodness knows how many kilos of drugs in the garage! Said he didn't know what was in them. Can you believe that?!"

"And you didn't believe him?" Guy's voice was quiet, small. He realised the letter which was still in his right hand was shaking like the last leaf of autumn. He dropped it onto the tabletop and placed his hands flat on either side of it.

"Oh, I wanted to. At first, anyway. But the police had all this evidence. There was no getting away from it. Your father was in it up to his neck, all the others turned on him, gave him up." She took another large gulp of wine. She was calmer now, the anger giving way to sadness.

"I have to go and see him, Mum."

She stared at him for the moment, her eyes burning, before turning away and refilling her glass.

"NOW DON'T FREAK OUT," Laura said as soon as Brock stepped through the door of their house.

"Well that's never something someone wants to

hear as they arrive home, is it?" he said as he hung his coat on the rack on the wall.

"I just know what you're like," she said, standing on tiptoes to kiss him lightly on the cheek. "Any sort of change and you act like the world's ended."

"And how exactly do you know how I'd react to the world ending?" he said as he followed her along the hall to the kitchen.

She stopped and turned to him, her head tilting to one side as she frowned.

"Actually, you're right. I think you'd enjoy the world ending. It would give you something new to moan about, and it would give you the chance to say you were right about all the things you already moan about."

He tried to form a hurt expression but instead burst out laughing.

"Right, now you're in a good mood," she said, pushing open the kitchen door.

There was a scrabbling of claws on the laminate wood floor and a small, scruffy bundle of brown slid straight into Brock's legs, where it proceeded to tug at his shoelaces.

He stared downward for a moment as the small puppy growled and pulled at his shoes. He looked up to see Laura, a worried and apologetic smile on her face.

"Look, I know we should have talked about this first," she said, her hands spread in front of her apologetically. "But I thought it would be difficult to deal with a puppy and a baby at the same time, so if we got the puppy now, then it would be all house trained and things by the time the baby arrived."

Brock felt his chest heave. "You mean...?" he said, his voice breaking.

"Oh." Laura's eyes widened in horror as she realised how what she had said had sounded. "Oh no, I'm not."

Brock breathed out slowly and watched her eyes fill with sudden tears. He moved forwards and hugged her closely.

"I think it's a fantastic idea. What's her name?"

"It's a boy, you idiot." She pushed him away and bent down to pick up the pup. "We can call him whatever we want, but the people at the rescue place were calling him Indy."

"Indy?" Brock said, taking the small bundle from her and holding it up to his face. The dog had spaniel ears, but long rangy legs that seemed too large for its body. It was clearly a cross-breed of some sort.

"Did they say what the breed was?" he asked as the puppy sniffed at his hands.

"A working cocker spaniel and a border collie

mix apparently, which means he'll be intelligent and need lots of walking."

Brock glanced past the puppy and raised his eyebrow at Laura.

"Oh, we'll work it out," she said dismissively, moving closer and putting her arm around him. "Just look at his little face!" She stroked under the puppy's chin with one finger and its tail wagged enthusiastically.

"Indy," said Brock thoughtfully. "It's a good name, I think."

"Me too."

They were standing with her arm around him, staring at their new charge. Brock felt a warm glow take over him as he wondered if by some miracle they would be standing like this with a child one day.

A small noise made him look down to the see the puppy spraying him with urine.

"Oh, bloody hell!" he cried, putting the dog back onto the floor.

"I think that means he likes you," Laura said, laughing.

CHAPTER SIX

Poole paused while putting his trousers on as he caught sight of himself in the full-length mirror that leaned against the wall of his bedroom. His hand reached down and traced along the rough line of the scar that ran around the outside edge of his left thigh.

There was a time, before his fifteenth birthday, when he would have considered a scar from a bullet wound to be the absolute height of coolness. Now he avoided looking at it. Every time he did, the pain of that day came flooding back. He snapped his eyes from it and pulled his trousers on.

Half an hour later he arrived at the car park at Bexford Station to find the place alive with activity.

News vans, TV cameras and people with recording devices were gathered around the entrance to the building like lions around a zebra.

He readied himself for the onslaught of questions as he approached the front door. Keeping his eyes fixed firmly ahead, he used his long stride to eat up the ground quickly.

Roughly halfway through the throng, he slowed and looked about. No one had thrust a microphone in his face and asked him for a comment, no one had stuck a camera in his way. In fact, no one was even looking at him.

He continued, feeling slightly hurt at this response.

"You made it through all right then, I see?" Roland Hale said, his large belly half resting on the reception desk in front of him.

"Yes thanks, Roland," Poole answered, hoping he hadn't been watching the indifference of the press towards him through the window.

"Inspector Brock barely made it through a few minutes ago," Roland continued, a gleam in his eye. "They wouldn't leave him alone! Shouting questions at him, they were."

"Right," Poole said, teeth gritted.

Why on Earth did this bother him so much? They hadn't pestered him as he'd come in, so what? It didn't mean anything.

It did mean something, though. It meant they didn't see him as anyone of importance, or as someone who would know anything. He knew he was young for his position, but it got under his skin that people would judge him by his age.

He walked straight to the canteen and grabbed a coffee before joining Brock at his usual table in the corner of the small room.

"Morning, sir," he said as the inspector slid his empty plate to one side and picked up his own coffee.

"Morning, Poole."

Poole's eyes landed on the plate where the tell-tale signs of egg yolk and grease showed a fried breakfast had recently been devoured.

Laura, the inspector's wife, had given Poole strict instructions to make sure that her husband stuck to the diet he was on to increase his fertility and their chances of conceiving. Poole had, of course, said that he wasn't going to be an informant, and the three of them had all had a good laugh.

Despite Poole's refusal, Brock was now acutely aware that he knew about the diet he was supposed to be on and was forever looking guilty and furtive whenever Poole and food were around.

"Nice breakfast, sir?" Poole said innocently, his face blank.

"Yes thanks, Poole," the inspector said stiffly. "I suppose you came through that bloody scrum out there?"

"I did." Poole nodded. "Not surprising I guess. This is going to be headline news for a while yet."

"Which means we need to solve this as soon as possible before Bexford becomes a bloody circus," Brock grunted. "Bloody Ron Smith," he said, shaking his head. "He's got a lot to answer for here, even if he didn't kill anyone."

Poole frowned. "You don't really think he could have done it, do you?"

"Oh, I'm sure he didn't; he's too much of a weasel to actually hurt anyone. But I'll never rule anyone out unless it was impossible for them to have done it."

"So, what are you thinking?"

"I'm thinking that almost every one of those buggers last night gave us nothing, so I say it's time to do a little bit of digging, and I know just the person to help us." He nodded towards the door where Constable Davies was entering, his helmet lopsided as always.

"Morning, sirs," he said, grinning. "Isn't it exciting? All the press here and that."

"Oh, I can barely contain my excitement," Brock answered bitterly. "I hear you're a big fan of *Foul Murder*?"

"Yes, sir," Davies answered, looking embarrassed. "I know it's a bit silly and all that, but it's good fun."

"The real question is, what do you know about the actors?"

"Oh, well," Davies said, sitting down. "You've got Jarvis Alvarado, of course." He paused, frowning. "Well, did have, I guess. Anyway, he's the big star. My mum fancies him something rotten. She phoned me in a right state this morning when she found out."

Poole glanced at the inspector, waiting for an eye roll, but it didn't come.

"And what about gossip?" Brock said between sips of coffee. "What did this lot have going on in their private life?"

"Oh well, there's Jonny Turnbull's thing with the photographer, and then there's—" Davies stopped as Brock raised his hand.

"What photographer thing?"

"He punched a photographer a few weeks ago outside his house and someone got it on film. It was all over the internet." He looked at Brock's blank expression and turned to Poole for help.

"I have no idea what you're talking about," he said, palms raised.

This was true. While he watched the show, he had no idea about anything to do with the cast beyond their names.

He had never been into the world of celebrity,

and from the expression on the inspector's face, he wasn't either.

"OK," Davies continued slowly, "so Jonny Turnbull is your typical bad boy. He's been in rehab a couple of times; likes to party a bit too much apparently."

"And he's obviously got a temper?" Poole said.

Davies laughed. "Famous for it. He's always kicking off in some club or other."

"And what about Isabella Lennon?" Brock asked.

"She's was one of those 'it' girls." Again he looked at their blank expressions. "It's someone who's famous for being famous." Again, nothing from his audience.

"Let's just pretend that someone being famous for being famous makes sense and move on, shall we?" Brock said.

"Well, I don't know a lot about her other than she came from some rich family and was always in the papers, having her photo taken at parties. Then she got the job on *Foul Murder* and it was big news because it was her first acting job."

"Well, that explains her hamming it up in her interview with us, sir," Poole said. "She was still practising."

The inspector chuckled and then drained the last of his coffee. "OK, what about Eli Patrick?"

"I don't know much about him," Davies said, frowning. "He's not in the papers much."

"And Gina Glover?"

Davies' face turned a light crimson as he grinned like a school kid. "Yeah, she's amazing." He seemed to suddenly realise who he was talking to and turned an even darker shade. "I mean, she's a very good actress," he said hurriedly.

"And is she one of these..." Brock paused, "'it' girls you talked about?"

"Gina? Oh blimey, no! She's classy, you can just tell. There's talk of her going into films, you know," he said with a knowing nod.

"OK, well thanks, Davies. You can go and get on now."

"Yes, sir," he said, standing. They watched him walk away, waiting for him to realise. He'd got halfway to the door before he turned back. Poole lifted his helmet from the table and held it up for him.

"Thanks, sir," he said with an embarrassed grin, before turning away again.

"I think he was only a minute or two from asking if we could get him an autograph," Poole said, laughing. "How did you know he was into all that?"

"Constable Sanders told me," Brock said as he heaved himself up. "Come on, let's go and see if the pathologist's got anything, then we can get back down to the theatre."

Poole nodded but didn't stand. "Sir?"

Brock froze and looked back at him.

Guy Poole had a face that always appeared at least slightly worried. His forehead had the lines of a man twice his age. Now though, there was a different complexion to it.

"You've heard from your father?" Brock said, sitting down once more. His voice was flat, but his grey eyes were lit with an intense fire.

"I got a letter from him." He pulled the letter for his jacket and slid it across the table.

Brock took it, unfolded it and read it in silence before sliding it back to him.

"You need to go," he said.

Poole looked at him in surprise.

"Look," Brock said, noticing his reaction. "I know I haven't known you very long, but it's clear what happened with your father is still in your head, and it always will be until you meet him face to face and hear what he has to say."

Poole looked down at his hands as he picked at a stray piece of skin to the side of one nail.

"It sounds like he wants to convince me he's innocent," he said, leaving the words hanging there.

"Well, let him," Brock answered. "If he convinces

you, you've got your dad back. If he doesn't, at least you can properly move on."

Poole nodded but didn't really agree. The inspector made it all seem so simple, just a binary matter to be decided, black or white.

It wasn't like that in his mind. He was confused, angry, and uncertain. He wasn't even sure what he would feel if his dad did convince him he was innocent, though he could see no chance of that.

He thought of his friend Simon who had died that day. He thought of blood.

"Come on," Brock said, standing again. "Let's get on with the case, take your mind off it."

Poole gave him a weak smile and followed.

CHAPTER SEVEN

"I have to say, this really is quite exciting," Todd Peel said, his long fingers interlocking on the desk in front of him. "I mean, the facilities here are really quite excellent, and to be brought in on this case—well!" A wide smile spread across his thin lips.

"I'm very pleased for you," Brock said. "But can we just hear what you've found?"

Todd frowned and shuffled some papers in front of him. "Well, yes, of course, but I'm afraid there isn't much to say."

"It will be nice and brief then, won't it?" Brock said, leaning forwards.

Poole looked at him, starting to wonder whether it was Ronald Smith the inspector had a dislike for or just all pathologists.

"Mr Alvarado was killed by blunt force trauma

to the skull. I'm not able to say with any accuracy what the weapon might have been, but it was something hard, heavy, and it had a slightly rounded edge."

"A pipe? Some sort of bat maybe?"

"Possibly." Todd nodded. "But the wound was rather narrow, and there's something else."

"Yes?"

Todd Peel picked up a blue, decorative glass ball from a small tray of pebbles and pointed to the side of it with a pencil.

"Well the wound was across the top of the head." He drew an imaginary line across the top of the glass ball. "The blow came from a high angle. At first, I thought this meant that we were looking for a tall perpetrator, but then I realised."

They waited, but Todd Peel simply smiled at them.

"Realised what?" Brock barked impatiently.

"That this injury could also have been delivered by something swinging." He leaned back, looking pleased with himself.

Brock narrowed his eyes. "You mean like something swung over someone's head?"

"Well, yes," Todd said, leaning forwards again. He looked for all the world like a man who had had his thunder stolen.

"But you say the object would have had to be heavy?" Brock continued.

"Yes, definitely."

"OK, let us know if you find anything else," the inspector said, standing.

"Um," Todd said as they reached the door.

They turned back to him.

"I have had rather a lot of calls from the press, I'm afraid."

"Just ignore them, don't tell them anything."

Todd nodded.

"And I'm afraid Ronald Smith has been calling me asking me for details as well."

Brock exhaled through his nose. "I'll talk to him," he said and stepped through the door.

POOLE LEFT Brock calling Ronald Smith in the car park. Although the inspector had moaned about Smith not following his instructions by staying out of the case, Poole had noticed he had also seemed quite pleased at the idea of an excuse to read him the riot act.

Poole ran up the steps to the station, pleased to see that the press had moved on while they had been in the pathologist's office. Earlier, he had noticed again that as he and Brock had had left the station to cross the car park to the council offices, he had been ignored. The few press members who had been left at that time threw questions at Brock, who gave them a stone-faced silence in return.

"Did you see they've gone?" Roland said from behind the reception desk as Poole entered the building.

"I did," Poole said, noting that Roland had a strange, knowing smile on his face.

He swiped his security card and moved through the door and into the main office.

"Well, well," a familiar, loud voice said almost as soon as he was through the threshold. "If it isn't the copper to the stars."

Anderson leaned against a desk and folded his arms. "What's it like being a celebrity officer then, Poole?" he boomed, loud enough so that everyone in the office heard.

"Fine, apart from the stupid questions from idiots," Poole shot back. Anderson straightened up and stared at him as he walked along the aisle between desks.

"Oh, very clever. I guess you think you're a big shot now, eh?"

Poole stopped next to him. "No, I think I have a murder to solve—and if I'm not mistaken, so do you?"

"Oh, don't worry about me, Poole. I know my job. The question is, can you do yours?"

Poole moved past him, shaking his head as the rest of the office turned back to their work.

He headed straight through to the canteen and the battered old coffee machine.

"You and Anderson are starting to become a regular double act," Sanita said from behind him as pressed the button to pour the first cup.

"It's not a show I want to be a part of, believe me." He felt an involuntary smile spreading across his lips as he turned to look at her face. She had large, bright eyes and a cheeky, lopsided grin that made his knees weak.

"How are you, Constable?"

"I'm good, sir." Her face hardened. "I've been helping Anderson and Sharp on their murder case."

"Oh right. A young woman, wasn't it?"

"Yes, sir, found smashed over the head." She took a deep breath. "Terrible."

"Do they have many leads?"

"Nothing," she said blankly. "We know she was working as an escort."

"An escort? In Bexford?" Poole said, surprised.

Sanita laughed. "Yes, even in Bexford. Anyway, according to her agency, she hadn't been working that night and we can't seem to find anyone who knew what she was up to. Her friends weren't with her at any rate."

"Well I hope they find whoever did it," Poole said taking the second cup of coffee. "I better get these back to Brock. See you later, Constable."

"Bye, sir." She grinned at him and turned away.

CHAPTER EIGHT

When closed, the theatre had a different feel. It was like an animal in hibernation, lifeless even. The seats lurked in the gloom like faceless spectators, and the cold of the large space sent a shiver down Poole's back as he crossed to the middle of the stage. The inspector strode before him, his large head scanning the wood-boarded area.

"It's quite a way from the wings to the centre of the stage," he said, as he halted at the spot where Jarvis Alvarado had died.

"It would be difficult to get all the way onto the stage, whack him over the head, and then get out in time in the pitch black Sir," Poole said, looking at the distance.

"Not just that," Brock said, folding his arms.

"Uniform have searched the surrounding area and there's no sign of a murder weapon."

"So, you think it must be still in the theatre?" Poole asked.

Brock looked at him, the corner of his mouth rising slightly. "It seems like it. The problem is there's probably a million places to stash something here."

They both gazed around the space, which was covered in more shadow than light.

"Bloody hell, it could be anywhere," Poole said, half under his breath.

"Actually, I don't think so," Brock said. "I think we can rule out anyone from the audience climbing up and killing him. They would have to either have the murder weapon on them, which seems like it would have been something people would have noticed, or dumped it back near where they were sitting. Uniforms have already checked everyone in the audience as they left, and they've looked under and on every seat in the house. No sign of anything."

"So that narrows it down to the people who were backstage, then?" Poole said, feeling slightly more optimistic about the whole thing.

"It does," Brock replied. "Uniform haven't found anything there either, though. There's a big storage room underneath the stage, but nothing. It's all a bit of a mystery, isn't it?" he said, turning to Poole, smiling. "Come on;, let's have a look around the place."

He turned and headed off towards the far side of the stage. The space beyond the well-worn wooden boards of the stage gave way to dusty concrete, lined with a brick wall. Tools and pieces of rope hung from black hooks, and a ladder ran up into the gloom. The whole place had the feel of a handyman's garage rather than a place of performance.

They moved towards the back of the stage where the area curved round towards the far side. A corridor stretched away to the left and Brock headed down it with Poole following.

"So, this is where the stars hang out," Poole said, looking at the doors on either side of the hall, each with the words "dressing room" and a number on them.

"Does it make you wish you'd taken up a different vocation, Poole? Just think, you could have been a star on *Foul Murder* yourself."

"I doubt it, sir. I can barely convince anybody I'm a detective, let alone something I'm not."

The inspector paused and looked at him.

Poole felt his cheeks redden. "The media didn't ask me any questions this morning when I came in. It bugged me a bit. Sorry—just being stupid."

"Never mind, Poole," Brock said, slapping him on

the shoulder. "They'll be all over you from now on."

"Oh? Why, sir?"

"Well, now they've seen you with me, haven't they?" He smiled at Poole, who was trying to stop his eyes from rolling. "Right," Brock said, clapping his hands together. "Let's get you running, shall we?"

"Running?"

"We have to start working out the timings on all this, don't we? Apparently the lights were out for three minutes, so we need to see who could have got to the stage, whacked Jarvis over the head and then got back to where they were standing."

"So you want me to run to see if I can make it there and back in that time from where everyone backstage was standing?"

"Only one person, really. Mike Hart."

Poole's eyebrows rose. "You think he's our killer?"

"I think everyone's our killer until I can prove otherwise," Brock answered. "But this time I was actually thinking about saving your legs. Mike Hart was the farthest person away backstage, so if you run from where he was and make it, we know they could all have done it."

Poole sighed and walked to the far end of the corridor, which ended in another wall.

"Well, I might as well start at the farthest point that he could have been standing," he said, turning around again. "He said he was on the phone in this corridor, right?"

"He did," Brock said, pulling the sleeve of his jacket back and looking at his wristwatch. "OK... go."

Poole burst into a run, moving down the corridor and out into the space beyond before diving left through the opening and onto the stage itself. He ran to the middle and, feeling foolish, swung an imaginary murder weapon over his shoulder onto an invisible victim, turned and ran back.

"How long was I, sir?" Poole said, panting, his hands on his knees.

"One and a half minutes. Not bad, Poole."

"Just a couple of problems, sir," Poole said, straightening up. "I wasn't actually carrying a sack with a heavy object in it which might have slowed me down. Also, it doesn't leave much time for the murderer to dispose of the weapon, does it?"

"No, it doesn't," Brock said.

A voice came from behind them. "Erm, hello?"

They turned to see Jane Marx standing holding a screwdriver, her skin pale, her expression as though she had had a nasty shock.

"Miss Marx? Everything OK?" Brock asked, moving towards her.

"I, um, I think I might have found something to do with the murder," she said hesitantly.

CHAPTER NINE

Jane Marx led them back down the corridor into the space behind the stage and pointed at four small openings in the wall set an equal distance apart from each other.

"You see these holes? Well, they go into a chute that leads down into the props room below. It's so you can quickly get stuff down there without having to all the way down."

Without waiting for them to ask why this was relevant, she turned and moved to the back of the stage on the far side.

There was no corridor here; the space just curved around to the opposite wing that they had come out of when they had arrived. There was, though, an opening in the floor—a large trapdoor that was open now and secured against the wall with a brass hook.

"Haven't uniform already looked down here, sir?" Poole said as Jane Marx began to descend a flight of wooden steps that ran down from the trapdoor.

"They did, but it wasn't open when the event was happening so I'm guessing they only gave it the once-over," Brock answered grimly, leaving Poole under no illusions that someone was going to get it in the neck for missing whatever Jane Marx had found.

They descended into a chaotic and overwhelming space. Large metal shelving units ran off into the distance and Poole estimated that the basement ran beyond the stage and at least halfway under the seating.

Jane Marx walked along the wall until she reached a metal chute that ended in a long-walled shelf.

"In here," she said, jerking her thumb towards it.

They moved to it and leaned over the small wall of the shelf. At the bottom was a cloth bag with a deep red stain at its base where something bulked through the material from the inside.

"Our murder weapon, sir," Poole said.

"Looks like it. Get Sheila on the phone; I want

her team down here as soon as possible. Take prints off the top of the chute."

He turned to Jane Marx who was standing, hands on hips, behind them. "Does anyone have access to down here?"

"Most of the backstage people who work here do, but everyone was cleared out for this event, so it was just me. I opened it yesterday for your lot to come down and then closed it up again until this morning. It doesn't really matter though, does it? I mean, someone clearly threw it down the chute."

Brock grunted his agreement and turned back to the sack.

"Do you recognise this sack? Is it something from the theatre?" he continued with his back turned.

Poole watched Jane smirk.

"There are a million things like that down here; just take a look around." She gestured to the shelves spreading away in the distance.

"Is there any way up onto the stage from down here?" Brock asked, suddenly turning back to her.

"Yeah, there's a trapdoor right in the middle. Works on hydraulics."

"Can you take us to it?"

She nodded and turned around, heading down the aisle directly behind her.

Though she was sullen and not overly talkative,

there was something Poole liked about her. She was relaxed and confident, as though nothing could faze her. She was also attractive. Lean and fit from her work around the theatre, she had an athleticism about her he couldn't help but admire.

"Here it is," she said as the shelving units vanished to reveal a large open space, dominated by a large mechanical arm that rose up to a square of the ceiling above them.

"Can you lower it for us?" Brock asked.

She nodded and moved across to a grey box on the wall. She flipped a large switch and a loud hum broke out, echoing around the confined space. She then pressed the lower of two buttons and the mechanical arm began to bend slowly, lowering the chunk of ceiling down with it. Other than the hum of the motor, the procedure was surprisingly quiet. They watched it in silence, feeling the cooler air from above rushing in as the platform descended. When it had reached the bottom, Brock stepped onto it and inspected the floor.

"Is that how slow it is generally to go up and down?"

"Yep," Jane replied. "Only two speeds and that was the fastest. It's for musical stuff really. You know, big entrances and exits rather than making someone disappear."

Brock nodded and stepped back off the platform. "You can raise it up again now."

Jane nodded and moved back to the switch.

"I don't think anyone could have had the time to either use this or the trapdoor, and the stairs to dump the sack," Poole said, moving closer to the inspector.

"Me neither," Brock answered in a low voice. "Which means whoever killed him dumped it down that chute. When Sheila gets here, I think we should have one more experiment with your running skills, Poole."

CHAPTER TEN

Poole was sitting on one of the five metal stools that had been arranged on the stage for the cast of *Foul Murder*.

"Are you ready?" Brock asked him, looking at his watch again.

"Yes, sir."

"Then go!" Brock said suddenly.

Poole leapt from the stool and headed for the wings. Diving backstage, he ran around the rear of the stage until he reached the chute. Again, he felt silly as he made the motions of pulling a sack from his pocket and throwing it down the chute, before turning and running back. He reached the stage again and jumped back onto the stool.

"Well, sir?" he said breathlessly.

"Fifty-five seconds," Brock answered grimly.

"So, they could have smuggled some sort of sack and weight in, run backstage, and dumped it down the chute before getting back before the lights came on," Poole said. "They must eat plenty of carrots."

"Carrots?" Brock looked at him, frowning.

"You know, to see in the dark, like you said before."

"Oh, right," Brock grumbled, clearly not in the mood for jokes. "Yes, the dark is a problem. I think we've had enough of looking at the physical side of things, now. Let's see if we can dig deeper into the fact that everyone seems to have hated this Jarvis chap, shall we?"

They headed back out of the theatre and into the Sinton Hotel next door.

The cast were arranged at the same table they had been the night before. Mike Hart leapt up from his seat and hurried across to them.

"Just what the hell is going on here, Inspector?" he shouted as he crossed the carpet towards them. "I was told that we could be let go today and yet here we still are, kept in this blasted place like criminals! These oafs of yours are running about the place like prison guards!"

"I have asked the uniformed officers to keep you here. They're just doing their job. I'm sure you and your group all want us to catch who murdered Jarvis Alvarado as soon as possible?"

"Well, of course," Mike said, a practised look of sad concern coming across his face. "But we're losing money just sitting here, a lot of money."

"Better to lose money than your life," Brock said gravely.

"Well, yes. Quite," Mike Hart said.

Brock looked over his shoulder at the group behind. "Where's Jonny Turnbull?"

Hart looked nervous. "No one's seen him this morning. Apparently he's pretty angry at being stuck here."

"Oh, is he now? Poole," Brock said, turning to him. "Go and get a uniform to check on him, will you?"

"Yes, sir."

Poole turned and made his way back out into the foyer of the hotel, where he saw Constable Sanders arriving through the large double doors.

"Hello, sir," she said. The smile on her face sent something fluttering in his chest.

"Hello, Constable. Are you just arriving?"

"Yes, taking over from Morgan."

"Well, before you do that, can you do me a favour?"

She placed her hands on her hips, which shifted to one side and caused Poole's throat to tighten.

"You're always asking favours, aren't you? Like when I had to help you clean toilet roll off your car."

"Ah, now technically I didn't actually ask you to help with that," he said, grinning.

"True. Maybe I just have a weakness for saying yes to things."

Poole wasn't sure, but he could have sworn that the temperature in the hotel had just risen by roughly one thousand degrees.

"Constable, I need you to see if Jonny Turnbull is still in his room."

He watched her face crack from the flirtatious smile into work mode. Crap. What the hell had he said that for? Why on earth hadn't he come back with some witty and flirty response that would have had her melting at the very sight of him?

Instead, he had talked to her like an inferior officer and brought them both thudding back to the reality of work.

"I'll find out what room he's in and go there, now," she said, moving off to the reception desk, a small bundle of efficiency.

Poole trudged back to the bar area, feeling slightly subdued.

He arrived back to find Brock sitting at the table

they had occupied last night, this time with Mike Hart sitting opposite him.

"Inspector, you can't expect me to sit here and gossip about these people," he was saying as Poole joined them. "I have to maintain a level of trust with these people. Besides, they're my friends."

Brock gave a snort. "Friends? Come on, Mr Hart, let's not all become actors saying lines, eh? These people aren't your friends, they're your meal ticket and you want to stay onside with them. I can understand that. But there's something you need to understand as well." The inspector leaned forwards, his elbows on the table. Poole watched as Hart's eyes widened and began to dart around, trying to take all of Brock in. It wasn't an easy task.

"One of these people could well have murdered your star performer in cold blood, right there in front of hundreds of people. Do you think someone like that would hesitate to make you next on their list?"

Mike Hart swallowed.

"Especially if they maybe thought you knew something—maybe something that could lead to their arrest?"

"But I don't!" Hart protested.

"Maybe, maybe not, but one thing's for sure: I could give the impression you had and see where it leads me." Brock's face broke into a grin. "I could use you as bait."

Mike Hart paled. "You—you can't do that!"

"Of course, you were also close enough to have run on stage and hit Jarvis while still having time to dispose of the murder weapon."

Hart's mouth hung open like a fish. He looked over his shoulder quickly at the table of actors, assured that none of them were paying any attention, and then spoke in a low voice.

"Look, if you want the truth, I wouldn't put it past any of this lot to have killed Jarvis. Actors are all bloody insane." He waved one hand as if to emphasise the point. "But if you want someone who really had a motive to kill him, then talk to Jonny Turnbull."

"Oh, and why's that?" Brock said, eyebrows rising.

"Well, Jarvis has just got the lead in a big budget British gangster film. It's all very hush-hush, of course." He looked at them both as though he had just revealed the location of the Holy Grail.

"And?" Brock said, unimpressed.

"Well, Jonny Turnbull was also given a role; he was going to be Jarvis' right-hand man in the film, but Jarvis scuppered it."

"How do you mean?"

"Jonny confronted him last week at rehearsals and was going crazy at him, saying he'd had a call from his agent and he was off the picture because Jarvis had had a word with the director. Called him all sorts of names and then launched himself at him. Luckily security was nearby, and they pulled him off before either of them did any damage, otherwise the whole opening could have been ruined."

"Yes, imagine that?" Poole said flatly. "Last night's big success could have all been for nothing."

Mike Hart's lips tightened in anger as he stared back at him. "Yes, well. I didn't know this would happen."

The three of them looked to their left as one. Constable Sanita Sanders had entered the bar and was moving purposefully towards them.

"He's not there, sir," she said, her voice tight and hard.

"Jonny Turnbull?" Poole said, looking between her and the inspector.

"Yes, sir. The door was locked and there was no answer, so I got the maid to let me in, but he's not in there. There are no signs of a struggle or anything, but..." She hesitated, biting her bottom lip as she did so. "Well, you better come and have a look."

She turned and headed back the way she'd come.

"Wait here with the others please, Mr Hart,"

Brock said as he hitched his trousers up and headed after her. It struck Poole as he followed him that for a man who was so large it was incredible he had loose trousers at all.

They headed up the sweeping staircase, which doubled back on itself as they went up another floor. Then they moved along a wide corridor, its plush carpet making the place eerily quiet as they reached the door of number forty-two, which was still slightly ajar.

"I hope you didn't leave a crime scene unattended, Constable," Brock said, pushing the door open and stepping inside.

"Not a crime scene exactly, sir," Sanita answered in a voice which barely disguised her annoyance at this slight.

The room itself was tastefully decorated and furnished, as you would expect from a high-class establishment such as the Sinton Hotel. A small sofa was positioned on the far side of the room next to the bay window and opposite a flat screen TV that hung on the wall. The large bed ended in a dark, carved wooden roll. A door to its right led to the bathroom.

"Well, what are we looking at, Constable?" Brock said as she followed them in.

"In the bathroom, sir," she said, pointing through the door.

Brock pushed it open and they stepped inside. Across the large mirror that was flat against the tiles on their left was a short sentence written in shaving foam.

It read:

I'M SORRY FOR WHAT I DID

"POOLE," Brock said quietly.

"Yes, sir?"

"Get crime scene up here, will you? I'm suddenly quite concerned for the safety of Jonny Turnbull."

CHAPTER ELEVEN

Brock and Poole watched as Sheila and her two assistants began to crawl across the apartment in their white suits, various sprays and utensils in their hands.

"Why do you think something might have happened to Turnbull?"

"You've met him," Brock said, turning to him. "Why do you think?"

Poole thought for a moment. "He wouldn't have left that message."

Brock smiled. "And why not?"

Poole began to talk, forming the words in his mind as he went.

"Jonny Turnbull is a hot-head with a short temper, and he's arrogant. Could he have flown off the handle in a fit of rage and killed Jarvis? I think so, yes. But could he have pulled it off in the cool, calculated way the killer must have used? It seems unlikely. I can't see him taking the time to stand and write that message before he ran for it, either. He would have just acted on impulse and ran, unless he was so full of remorse he felt he just had to, and that doesn't seem like him. In any case, running is a stupid move. He had no reason to think we were on to him for the murder, and he's got to be one of the most recognisable people in the country. Keeping a low profile isn't going to be easy with half the press looking for him as well as the police." Poole paused, realising he had gone on for longer than he had intended, but when he turned to the inspector it was to see him still smiling.

"Good, Poole, good," he said, nodding. "And I agree with you. I think something happened to Turnbull and I don't think it's good."

Sanita arrived back at their side from her trip back down to reception. "The hotel staff say they didn't see him leave through the front entrance, sir, but then there are quite a few people going in and out so they could have missed him."

Brock grunted, "Any other exits?"

"Yes, sir, there's a fire escape at the end of this corridor, leads down into the courtyard behind the hotel."

Brock turned to where she pointed a slender finger and headed towards the door at the end, a fire exit sign above it. Poole followed, nodding at Sanita and giving her a sympathetic smile as he passed.

He could see from the strained expression in her eyes that she was kicking herself for having left the room unattended. It may not have looked like a crime scene at the time, but the inspector had been clear that he thought it was. And at the end of the day, that was all that mattered.

In the short time he had known Sanita; he had found her warm, funny and, on the odd occasion, spiky. There was something else there though, underlying how she appeared on the surface. A lack of self-belief, perhaps? A way of being too hard on herself?

He followed the inspector out through the door and into a stairwell of crisp white walls and matching shining floors only broken by the grips on each step heading down.

As they descended, his mind strayed to Friday's potential meeting with his father. How would Sanita react if she knew what his father had done? Would she then question Poole as he sometimes did, wondering if the apple really didn't fall far from the tree?

They emerged through another door into a

courtyard lined with the back of buildings from the street on the other side. Several cars were parked around the edge.

"Some nice cars here," Poole said, looking around at the assorted Jaguars and Bentleys.

"What do you expect?" Brock replied. "This is the hotel of the stars these days," he said in a sarcastic voice. "Find out how Jonny Turnbull got here and, if he came by car, if it's still here."

He walked to the right where an archway led under part of the hotel and back out into the road. "Check any cameras we have in the area, see if we can find an image of him leaving."

"Yes, sir," Poole said, making a note of all this in his small black notebook.

"Let's go and put a bit of pressure on the rest of the cast, shall we?" Brock said with a steely glint in his eye.

CHAPTER TWELVE

Poole watched as Brock surveyed his audience. The cast, along with their producer, Mike Hart, were sitting in a semi-circle facing him.

"It appears that Jonny Turnbull has left this hotel. Do any of you know where he might have gone?"

There was a moment of silence before Eli Patrick spoke. "Oh, you know Jonny!" he said in a joking tone. "He's probably gone off with a female fan, if you know what I mean?" He looked around at his fellow actors, but no one else seemed to want to latch on to his rather obvious innuendo.

"And when was the last time you saw him, Mr Patrick?"

The smile flickered on the broad, healthy face of Eli. "Oh, um, I think I saw him last night at the bar."

"You think?" Gina Glover said, turning to him. "You were sitting at the same table."

"Oh, yes. Of course," Eli stammered, the smile now replaced by a look of anger towards Gina, who gave him a quick "you're welcome" smile.

"And when did you last see Mr Turnbull, Miss Glover?"

"When I saw him with Eli in the bar," she replied coolly. "He was moaning about being stuck in the hotel and saying how he was going to get out of here. I'm guessing he did."

"And was anyone else in the bar at that time?"

"Just me and Isabella," she said, gesturing to the thin, sallow-faced woman next to her.

"Is this true, Miss Lennon?"

"Of course it's true!" Isabella said, waving a hand in annoyance. "Bloody hell! How long are you going to keep us here answering these ridiculous questions? No wonder Jonny legged it."

"And what about you, Mr Hart?"

Mike Hart looked around at the cast and then back to the inspector. "I saw Jonny last night as well, in his room."

Brock raised an eyebrow. "What time was this?"

"Oh, around eight, I'd say?"

"And what did you talk about?"

Again, Hart's eyes flicked across to the others.

"I don't really think this is the time," he said, his cheeks flushing.

"Oh, come on, Mike. We're all friends here, aren't we?" Gina said with a malevolent smile on her lips.

Mike looked back at Brock and Poole with his chin raised defiantly. "I was talking to him about an upcoming movie deal." His eyes darted to his right and the rest of the crew.

"You absolute worm," Gina said, all signs of amusement gone from her deep brown eyes. "So, you were quite happy to jump straight to Jonny and set him up with some sweet deal that you'd take a cut from, but not me?"

"I've told you, Gina, you were not right for the role."

"Not right for the role? I'm right for any bloody role, Mike," she said, her voice full of venom.

"Rather than questioning us," Isabella said, "why aren't you talking to that funny little man who was always hanging around? He was here earlier today."

Poole glanced at Brock and saw his face cloud.

"Do you mean Ronald Smith, the medical consultant for the show?"

"Yes, that's the little twerp," Isabella confirmed. She reached out for her glass, which Poole noticed was filled with white wine despite the hour.

"Actually, I did see Ronald this morning in the foyer," Mike Hart said. "He was talking to the reception desk about something as I was going down to breakfast."

Brock reached into his pocket. It may have been the expression etched onto the inspector's face, or just that Poole had watched too many episodes of *Foul Murder*, but for a split second he was convinced he was going to pull a gun and start blasting at them all. Instead, he pulled a small stack of business cards and handed one to each of the actors, and finally to Mike Hart.

"Right now, all of you are suspects in a murder investigation. There is not a chance of any of you getting on with your lives until this is resolved. The best way we can all move on is if we find the killer, so I suggest you call me as soon as anything becomes clear." He paused and looked at them, waiting until all eyes were definitely on him. "For instance, if you suddenly had a flash of insight as to why one of your colleagues may have had reason to kill Jarvis Alvarado." He turned and left so suddenly that, for a moment, Poole was left gaping like the rest of them at this undisguised attempt to get them to turn on each other.

He turned and hurried to the lobby door after

Brock, as voices of recrimination and swearing broke out behind him.

"Is that wise, sir?" he said as he joined him, standing in the middle of the lobby. "I mean, if someone did do something to Jonny Turnbull for some reason, it means there's someone seriously dangerous here, someone who's willing to do whatever it takes to cover their tracks. And now you've turned them on each other?"

"We're going to position officers in the corridors tonight," Brock said without looking at him. "I'll make sure they're safe. These people, though..." He shook his head. "None of them can be bothered to tell us anything that might be of use, and the only thing I have to leverage them with is the fact that they're stuck in this hotel. So, I'm going to use it."

Poole nodded. He never seemed to be able to predict the inspector's next move. He was still trying to work him out, see what made him tick. He suspected he might well be trying to figure him out for the rest of the time that they worked together. There was something hard there, an edge to the man that was as formidable as his towering frame. Yet at other times he had an almost puppy-like quality.

"A bloody puppy," Brock said, making Poole jump. He had zoned out for a moment and hadn't heard what the inspector had said.

"A puppy, sir?" Poole said, the worrying thought that the inspector could read his mind bouncing around his head.

"Yes, Poole, aren't you listening? Laura's gone and bought a bloody puppy."

"Oh," Poole said with relief. "Well, that's nice."

"Is it?" Brock said gruffly. "Come on, I need a sandwich from Sal's and we need to talk to Ron again, find out what he's been up to."

He strode off towards the door and Poole followed in a state of confusion.

CHAPTER THIRTEEN

"And here you go!" Sal said, placing two enormous sandwiches in front of them. "Something special for my two favourite customers!" She beamed at them and placed her hands on her hips.

Poole reached down to lift one half of the sandwich and golden egg yolk dribbled from one side. He bit into it quickly and, eyes wide, nodded enthusiastically at Sal.

"He likes it!" she said, clapping her hands together. "Now let me get you some coffee." She turned and vanished back behind the counter.

Brock was already tucking into his sandwich with the ferocity of a bear who had found the salmon hard to come by for a while.

The sandwich consisted of bacon, sausage, black

pudding, and egg and was finished with a thin layer of béarnaise sauce. It was heaven.

Sal returned with their two coffees and they nodded their thanks rather than stop eating. When they'd finished, they leaned back, allowing their stomachs some room to breathe, and sipped at their coffee.

"So, are you the only person in the entire world who doesn't like puppies?" Poole said, continuing the conversation that had fizzled out as they'd left the hotel in the search for food.

Brock took a deep breath and stared out of the window. "I love dogs," Brock said. "I've been talking about getting one for ages."

"So, what's the problem?"

Brock's grey eyes latched themselves onto Poole's. "The problem is that we've talked about getting a dog for so long, why has Laura suddenly decided we should buy one now, just a few weeks after I came clean about my lazy swimmers?"

Poole flinched slightly. Brock's openness around personal matters still caught him off guard, made him feel ill at ease—particularly when referring to his superior's low sperm count.

He was still not comfortable talking about his own problems, about his father, but the inspector seemed to have no such worries. It struck Poole that

Brock used his partners as a kind of sounding board, both for the police work they did and for his personal life.

"You think she's maybe got the puppy because she thinks you won't be able to have children?"

Brock grunted an agreement. "Compensating."

"Maybe she just thinks it's the right time?"

"Maybe," Brock said. A sudden smile crept across his face. "Funny little thing, he is. Dark brown apart from his legs, which are white. Looks like he's got socks on."

Poole smiled, seeing the warmth in the inspector's expression. He imagined him being a father for the first time and it struck him that he'd be a great one.

Unlike his own.

He looked out of the window as his thoughts drifted back to his meeting with his father which he realised, like a punch in the gut, was now tomorrow.

"Ready for tomorrow?" Brock said, watching him carefully.

"I'm not sure it's something you can get ready for, sir," Poole said, his gaze still scanning the street outside.

"And where are you meeting him?"

"The Market Wine Bar."

"What time?"

Poole turned to him, a suspicious look in his eyes. "Sir?"

"Don't you think it might be a good idea if you had someone there with you? I'm assuming your mother won't want to go. I can be there."

Poole felt a sudden overwhelming rush of emotion. It rose up through his chest like a wave of hot lava and threatened to burst across his face in the form of red-hot tears. This man, who he had only known a few months, was willing to be there as he confronted his father, was willing to be there for him in a way that that man had not been since he was fifteen.

He fought the feelings back by draining the last of his coffee hurriedly and sitting up in his chair.

"Thank you, sir. That's very kind, but I think this is something I should probably do alone."

He looked up at Brock's grey eyes, which seemed to be staring right through him to the back of his skull.

"Well, if you need me," he said in a low voice.

"Thank you," Poole said, feeling awkward now. He idly stirred the last dregs of his coffee with his spoon until Brock's phone rang out with the song Gangnam Style. The inspector rolled his eyes as Poole laughed, knowing that the inspector's wife Laura had again changed his ringtone. Brock was so useless with technology that he had no idea how to change it back to something more sensible.

"Hello?" he said, placing the receiver to his ear. His eyebrows rose as someone spoke on the other end of the line and he looked at Poole, a smile playing on his lips.

"OK, go on," he said before pulling the handset away from his ear and gesturing wildly to Poole to put it on loudspeaker. Poole took the device and pressed the correct button, which resulted in the voice of Eli Patrick barking from the small speaker.

"Hello? Are you still there?"

"Yes," Brock replied with a wide smile. "I'm here. What was it you needed to tell us, Mr Patrick?"

There was a slight pause from the other end of the phone. The only sound was a barely audible sign hissing gently through the handset.

"I think you should speak to Isabella about her and Jarvis."

"What do you mean?" Brock asked, glancing at Poole.

"I mean that a couple of nights before the launch they were shacked up together. I saw Isabella leaving his hotel room first thing in the morning, and she was still in same clothes as the night before."

"And why didn't you share this information with us before, Mr Patrick?"

"Look, everyone knows that Jarvis was getting this big film role, and he had a lot of sway with the directors about his supporting cast. I wasn't about to rock the boat with him," he said, his clipped, well-spoken voice diving lower. "Everyone pretty much hated the guy, but he could have been the key to any of us making it into films. He knew it too, enjoyed the fact that everyone was suddenly fawning over him."

"And you think he used his influence to seduce Isabella?"

A braying laugh burst from the speaker. "Isabella wouldn't need seducing; she'd do anything to advance her career."

"Well thank you, Mr Patrick. Please come back to me if anything else comes to mind regarding Jarvis' death."

"Oh, right, yes," the voice said as Brock gestured at Poole to hang up.

Poole pressed the button and looked up. "So, Isabella was having a fling with Jarvis? Funny she didn't mention it, eh?"

"And it's also funny that none of them decided to mention that Jarvis could well have been their meal ticket. The question is, who did Jarvis let down that made them angry enough to kill?"

"Who was that lovely young man on the phone?"

Sal said, moving from behind her counter. "Lovely voice, he had. He sounded like a nice boy."

"Oh? What makes you say that?" Poole asked.

"There are people who have voices like that who can be cruel people, arrogant."

"You mean because he's posh?" Poole said, smiling at her.

Sal smiled back. "Money doesn't make people kind," she said with a tilt of her head.

She turned and headed back behind the counter with their now empty coffee cups.

"I can see you don't just come here for the sandwiches, but the personality insights too," Poole said, watching her head back through the door behind the counter.

"Come on," Brock said, laughing, "let's go and see Ron. Then I want to get back and see if they've turned anything up at the hotel on Jonny Turnbull, and I think we'll have a little chat with Isabella Lennon again."

Brock got up and then paused, frowning.

"Best not to mention our little visit here to Laura, eh, Poole?" he said, avoiding Poole's eyes.

"Of course, sir," Poole answered dutifully, trying to hide a smile.

"I'M SORRY, Sam, but my career is on the line here!" Ronald Smith wailed. "No, not just my career, my life!"

"So, you thought you'd help put yourself in prison by messing up my investigation, did you?"

"I was just asking a few questions!"

"You were hanging around a place you had no right to be, and talking to suspects in a murder inquiry that you yourself are a suspect in!" Brock roared.

Ronald Smith visibly wilted under the onslaught. "Oh, it's all such a mess!" he cried, rubbing his hands over his bald head.

He slid down in the cheap wooden chair he was sitting in. When Brock had called Ronald to meet, he had apparently been having a late breakfast at a supermarket café—trying to fill his time now that he had no work to go to. Poole had felt a pang of sadness for the little bald man upon hearing this.

"What were you doing at the hotel earlier?" Brock asked, his voice level again.

"I was just trying to find out what was going on! You wouldn't tell me," he said accusingly. "You just told me to stop calling that Todd Peel idiot who's sitting in my bloody office."

Poole noticed a softening of Brock's face. "And did you find anything out?" the inspector asked.

"No," Ronald replied miserably. "Just that all the cast have done is sit there and drink since it all happened."

"Look, just leave this to us, OK?" Brock said. "We'll have you back behind your desk and being a pain in my arse before you know it."

Ronald looked up at him and blinked. "Thank you, Sam."

"Don't mention it," Brock said, standing up to leave. "But if I catch you messing about and asking questions again, I'll put you in a cell just to keep from incriminating yourself."

Ronald nodded and pushed at the leftover crumbs of his croissant.

CHAPTER FOURTEEN

Refuelled by the high calorie count of their sandwich, the pair arrived back at the hotel to find it a hive of activity. Various uniformed officers milled around the foyer, and Sheila Hopkins, the crime scene manager, standing and giving instructions to a couple of her colleagues.

"Anything, Sheila?" Brock asked, striding across to her.

"Nothing, Sam. Well, other than a million fingerprints from everyone who's stayed here recently. They don't clean as much as you'd expect for a place that charges as much as they do," she said, smiling.

"There was nothing from his room?" Brock snapped, not in the mood for jokes after hearing Sheila and her team had come up with nothing.

"No," she said, straight-faced now. "The only fingerprints relating to anyone involved in the case in the room were Jonny Turnbull's. Even the can of shaving foam used to write the message only had his on."

Brock frowned. "So, it was obviously his shaving foam, but someone else could have worn gloves to write the message. And there were no signs of a struggle?"

"No, nothing unusual at all."

Brock breathed heavily out of his wide nose, putting Poole in mind of a snorting dragon.

"I'll see if uniform have pulled anything from the CCTV in the area," he said, moving towards a small group near the reception desk that contained the familiar faces of Constables Davies and Sanders.

Brock nodded and continued to talk to Sheila as Poole headed off, hoping to find good news.

"Oh, sir!" Davies said as Poole came up alongside him. "Sorry, we didn't know you were back." The young officer glanced nervously at Sanita next to him. Davies had a head that seemed to have stretched from front to back, making his face protrude somewhat. His Adam's apple bobbed as he talked.

"We checked the footage from the hotel's cameras. They've only got two working at the moment, one over the front door and one over the entrance to the car park. There's another one in the car park itself, but something went wrong with it last week and they haven't got it fixed yet. From the two we've looked at, it doesn't look like he left the hotel," Sanita said, her tone professional and impersonal, which somehow disheartened Poole as much as the news that there was still no clue as to Jonny Turnbull's whereabouts did.

"We've only whizzed through it so far, but Jones is going through it more thoroughly now. There are cameras in here as well," she continued, pointing to the two opposite corners of the large room. "But so far we haven't seen any sign of Turnbull."

Poole nodded, thinking hard. "Then he must be still in the building somewhere. We're going to have to do a room-to-room search. Can you find the manager and tell him that the inspector and I want to talk to him?"

"Yes, sir," Davies said, turning to go and immediately bumping into a crime scene operative who dropped a series of folders that scattered across the floor.

"Thank you, Constable," he said to Sanita, who replied with a short nod, a smile and a "sir".

He hovered for a moment without really knowing why. For some reason, the meeting with his father was looming in his mind, and he felt himself wanting to tell Sanita about it, to share his fear with her.

He turned sharply away and headed towards Brock, his long thin legs covering the distance quickly.

The manager of the hotel was a small, ferrety-looking man in an expensive-looking dark blue suit. Poole recognised him as Michael Johnson, brother of Terry Johnson, who ran the theatre next door, who they had met briefly when they had arrived to talk to the cast of *Foul Murder* yesterday.

"Officers, I really must object to the disruption that is being caused in my hotel this morning," he said as he and Poole arrived at the inspector together. "The cast of this television show are not our only guests."

"This is a murder investigation," Brock replied. "And I'll keep up with any disruption I deem necessary until it is solved."

"Jonny Turnbull is missing, and we have reason to believe he may have been harmed," Poole interjected before the hotel manager could argue further. "After checking the footage from your entrances we believe he is still in the building, so we're going to need to do a room by room search of the entire place."

Poole glanced slightly nervously at Brock. He

was springing this news on him and making the decision to conduct a search all at the same time, but the inspector merely raised his eyebrows and nodded in appreciation.

"People expect a certain level of service here at the Sinton Hotel. Just think what this is going to do to our reputation?" the man said pleadingly.

"I'm sure your guests will understand once it is explained to them that a serious crime may have been committed on the premises." There was a glint in Brock's stormy grey eyes, which seemed to make the small manager buckle.

"Of course. If you could be as discreet as possible, then I'm sure my staff would be able to assist you in carrying out the search in an efficient manner."

"Excellent," Brock said with a smile.

ISABELLA LENNON WAS SITTING on a small red sofa, her thin, bare legs crossed in front of her.

"So?" she said questioningly, her mouth caught between a pout and a sneer.

They had taken Isabella to her hotel room to question her on the late night stay she had had in Jarvis Alvarado's room.

"Well," Brock continued, "we can't help but wonder why you didn't tell us you were in a relationship with the deceased before."

"Because I wasn't." She shrugged. She saw their blank expressions, rolled her eyes and huffed in a way that would have graced any amateur dramatics performance. "If you're asking whether I slept with Jarvis then the answer is yes, but I wasn't in any kind of relationship with him." She laughed, a high and hard noise like breaking glass. "Maybe it's a police thing? Are you all prudes or something? No sex before marriage and all that?"

"And when exactly did this begin between yourself and Jarvis?"

"Just since we've been here. This place is the dullest little town I've ever been in. We were all bored out of our minds."

Poole noted the deliberate malice as she said this and felt the inspector tense slightly next to him at this attack on his town.

"And you were with Mr Alvarado the night before his murder?"

"Yes," she answered, sighing again.

"Did you notice anything odd about his behaviour?"

She gave another high laugh, like a bark from a

Pekinese. "Everything was odd about Jarvis' behaviour. The man was a spoiled brat."

Poole wondered for a moment if she could see the irony of saying this.

"Jarvis got a lucky break, and then he just took whatever he wanted and screwed everyone else, but that's the game isn't it?"

"The game?" Poole asked.

"Showbiz," she said with a shrug. "That's what it's all about. You reach up and grab whatever you can from above and at the same time you stamp bloody hard on whoever's below you."

Poole noticed Brock frowning at this surprisingly eloquent, if distasteful, point.

"And is that what you do, Miss Lennon?" Brock said, his voice hard and low. "You kick down the people below you and drag down the people above? Like Jarvis Alvarado maybe?"

"You know about the job?" she said, her cool suddenly evaporating.

Poole glanced at Brock, but his over-sized features were locked in a rigid, blank expression.

"I mean, everyone was all over him as soon as we knew about the movie deal." She looked up at them sharply. "But that's not why I slept with him. Jarvis was a good-looking bloke and I decided I needed a bit of fun. The fact that he might have been able to get me a role in the film was just an added bonus."

"And did he offer to put in a good word for you?"

"He said all the right things." She shrugged. "But who knew with Jarvis. He'd say anything if he thought he could get something out of you."

"And are you sure there isn't anything else you'd like to share with us?" Brock said, leaning forwards and placing his large elbows on his even larger thighs.

"Like?" she said, a mocking look in her eyes.

"Like maybe Jarvis promised you a role in the film, slept with you, and then told you to sod off because you had no chance of the role?"

Isabella's nostrils flared in anger as a knock came at the door of her hotel room.

Constable Davies came in, tripping over the doorframe as he did so.

"What is it, Davies?" snapped Brock, annoyed at the interruption.

"It's Jonny Turnbull, sir. We've found him."

From the frantic way his Adam's apple bobbed and the wide-eyed urgency in his eyes, Poole knew what he was going to say before the words had even left his lips.

"He's dead, sir," Davies finished with a squawk.

CHAPTER FIFTEEN

They found Gina Glover in the bar area, sitting at the bar itself with Mike Hart. Gina was swigging a large gin and tonic as Mike seemed to be pleading with her about something.

"Come on, Gina, be reasonable," he said as they approached.

"And what would you like Gina to be reasonable about, Mr Hart?" Brock said, his barking voice making the producer almost jump out of his black polo shirt. Poole had noticed that it was all the man ever seemed to wear, and for some reason, it irritated him.

Hart looked back at Gina, who gave a low laugh.

"He's trying to get me to change my mind."

"Change your mind about what?"

"I've quit the show. This series will be the last

Foul Murder I appear in. And good bloody riddance to it."

"Let's just not do anything rash," Mike Hart said. "We've all had a stressful couple of days. Let's just let the dust settle a bit."

"The dust settle?!" Gina shouted back at him, her face full of rage. "Jarvis is dead, and Jonny..." Her face turned to one of shock and she turned to Brock, who was standing to her left.

"Yes, Miss Glover? What about Jonny Turnbull?"

"Well, he's missing, isn't he?" she said, turning back to her drink and attacking it with gusto.

"No, Miss Glover, he's not missing," Brock said slowly.

Mike Hart's head jerked towards Brock, whereas Gina's remained staring at her glass.

"You've found him?" Hart said. "Where was he?"

"He was in the theatre," Brock said, his eyes not leaving Gina. "Isn't that right, Miss Glover?"

She turned to him slowly, her rich auburn hair falling across her left eyes slightly.

"I didn't kill him," she said in a flat, cold voice.

"What!" Hart said, slipping from his stool to his feet, his eyes wide. "Jonny's dead, too?"

"I'm afraid so, Mr Hart. But you knew that

already didn't you, Miss Glover?" Brock said, turning to her.

She drained the rest of her glass before speaking. "I'm not going to say another word without talking to my lawyer. But don't worry, Inspector; I've already called him, and he should be here at any moment."

"And at what point did you call him? Was it just after you'd killed Jonny Turnbull?"

"Inspector!" she said, her eyes wild. She looked as though she had more to say but stopped, instead taking a deep breath before she spoke more calmly.

"I'm not saying anything else until my lawyer is here. You can drag me down to the station if you want, but the same will apply and then you'll just have half the nation's press on your doorstep."

Brock eyed her for a moment before speaking, his eyes not leaving hers.

"Poole, go and find a constable to wait with Miss Glover until her lawyer gets here, will you? Then they can escort her to her room where we'll be along shortly."

Poole headed off to the lobby and returned a few minutes later with Constable Morgan, a sour-faced Welshman who always seemed to be chewing gum.

Gina smiled at him and turned back to the bar to order another gin and tonic.

"Can we have another word with you, Mr Hart?"

Brock said when Poole and his notebook had returned.

"Um, yes," Hart said, looking nervously at Gina.

They stepped towards the corner of the bar they had been sitting in on the first night, Brock's eyes constantly roving back to the bar where Gina was sitting with her back to them.

"Why is Gina Glover quitting the show?" Brock asked.

"Oh, I'm sure she won't quit; it's just all this business has put everyone on edge."

"It's also got two people killed," Brock said flatly.

"Yes," Hart said, his gaze dropping to the floor. "Jonny as well—I can't believe it."

"So what reason did Gina actually give you for quitting?" Brock said, not letting go of the thread.

Hart looked decidedly shifty. He half turned back to the bar, glancing at the back of Gina, then turned back to them, apparently satisfied she was far enough away.

"She seems to have got it into her head that she is being kept in the cold about this film deal," he said, his voice low and conspiratorial.

"This bloody film," Brock said shaking his head. "What exactly is it?"

"It's a full-length motion picture adaptation of the TV show. We have high hopes that it could become a long-running franchise, like James Bond or something."

"If it's based on the TV show, doesn't it make sense to just use all of the cast from the TV version?" Poole asked.

Hart looked at him as though he was a child asking a ridiculous question.

"There's a certain amount of concern from the company putting the film together that the current cast isn't quite... how shall I put this?"

"Not quite Hollywood enough?" Brock said, making Poole glance at him in surprise. This wasn't the first time in this case that the inspector had surprised him with his grasp of show business.

"Exactly," Hart said giving a slightly embarrassed smile. "Jarvis was fine, of course; he had that star quality everyone's looking for. In fact, the company were so keen for Jarvis to reprise the role he has on the TV show, they had asked him to consult on the rest of the casting. Somehow the rest of the cast here got wind of it and it caused some tension."

"What sort of tension?"

"Well there's something you've got to know about Jarvis," Hart said, his voice suddenly bitter and angry. "It wasn't about the job for him, or even the fame—it was about power. And having this sway with the movie deal put him over the edge. He was a bloody nightmare to everyone."

"So, you seem to be a man in the know. Who exactly was likely to be part of this film?" Brock said.

Hart's right hand began turning the wedding ring on his left absentmindedly. "To be honest, I don't really know." He looked slightly sheepish. The portrayal of being in control suddenly seemed slightly silly. He was scared now, his mind clearly revolving around the two deaths of his colleagues and deciding he didn't want to be any part of it all.

"I was playing them off against each other, trying to get some kind of idea of what was going on, so I could get in there myself somehow."

"And what did you find out?" Brock asked impatiently.

"Isabella was boasting about how Jarvis was going to get her a part in the film, so I tried to butter her up. But she told me to bugger off, and then Gina got wind of it and started having a go at me for helping to get Isabella a role instead of her." He put his head in his hands and rubbed his face hard.

"And what was Jonny's position in all of this?"

"Well, he..." Hart paused and looked up at them, something passing across his face as though a realisation had dawned. "Oh, bloody hell."

"What is it, Mr Hart?"

"When the news of Jarvis got out I got a phone call from the film company. Suddenly they actually did want me to get involved."

Poole noted the slight note of bitterness in his voice.

"I sort of suggested that maybe they could replace Jarvis with Jonny. His name is already linked to *Foul Murder* and I think given a break like this he could have gone on to big things."

"So, first Jarvis Alvarado is destined for the lead role and he's killed, then you suggest Jonny Turnbull and within a day he's dead too?" Brock said.

Mike Hart's face turned pale as he slumped back in his seat. "Oh God."

"And did you tell anyone else about this change of plan?"

"No. I wouldn't want to jeopardise the whole thing by blabbing my mouth off."

"Jonny Turnbull must have told someone," Poole said, turning to Brock. "And whoever that person is, they're likely to be our killer."

"Um," Hart said, frowning in confusion. "I doubt Jonny would have told anyone either for the same reasons, but that wouldn't matter anyway."

"How do you mean?" Brock said.

"Well everyone in the industry knows anyway—secrets don't stay secret for more than a few minutes in this job. Anyway, the main reason the film company were keen on appointing another member of the cast was precisely because Jarvis had been murdered. It's all good publicity, you see?"

"Bloody show business," Brock muttered darkly.

CHAPTER SIXTEEN

Brock and Poole had moved back towards the lobby area, deciding to catch up on whatever the early findings of Jonny Turnbull's death were.

As soon as they had passed through the swing door from the bar, they were confronted by the small and worried-looking figure of Ronald Smith.

"What the bloody hell are you doing here, Ron?" Brock said, his voice full of exasperation and annoyance. "Did you not understand what I said to you earlier?! You're really not doing yourself any favours."

"I know, Sam, but I need to talk to you." He looked around furtively. "In private."

"We're pretty busy right now, Ron. Can this wait until later?" Brock answered, looking past the small figure and scanning the room for someone who could give him an update.

"It's just that I've remembered something that happened the night before the launch."

Brock's eyes swung down and fixed on Ronald's.

"I'm not sure it's relevant to the case though," Ronald said hesitantly.

"Well that's not for you to decide now, is it?" Brock grumbled, his grey eyes intense. "Just tell us what you've remembered."

Ronald's small and almost hairless head turned left and right, his beady eyes searching the busy lobby. "Can we go somewhere else?"

Brock sighed impatiently but jerked a thumb towards the back of the hotel and headed off.

A few moments later, the three of them were standing in the courtyard at the back of the hotel as Ronald ran a hand across the top of his head. "The other night I saw Gina Glover and Jarvis going at it."

There was an uncomfortable silence.

"No!" Ronald shouted, his short arms waving above his head, "I don't mean like that. I mean they were arguing."

"Arguing? What about?"

"I don't know, but I caught a bit of what they were saying."

"Which was?" Brock asked impatiently.

"Look, Sam," Ronald continued in his whiny, nasal voice. "What the hell's going on here? I heard Jonny's dead too!"

"Ron, we don't know what's going on yet because every silly bugger involved in this bloody TV program isn't telling us everything they know, and now you're at it!"

"I just want to know I'm not going to be the next one to end up dead!"

"Then tell me what the hell you know, and maybe it will help catch who's done this!"

Ronald kicked at a stone on the floor, which rolled away and hit the wheel of a Jaguar. "Gina was saying something about Jarvis being ruled from his pants, and that he was being used by Isabella."

"And what did he say to that?" Poole asked.

"Well, he was angry. He told her she should stay out of it unless she was willing to change teams."

"Change teams?" Poole continued.

"Look, I don't know! That's all I heard!" Ronald said, his arms waving again. "Sam, you've got to do something about the press. They won't leave me alone—the phone at home hasn't stopped ringing and they keep coming around. They think I've been thrown off the case because I'm something to do with Jarvis' murder!"

"You've been thrown off the case because you *are*

something to do with his murder, Ron," Brock muttered as he moved past him and across the courtyard to the back door to the theatre. "You were there, it was your idea," he shouted over his shoulder. He stopped as he reached the doorway and turned back. "You've made this mess, Ron; now you're going to have to live with it until we can find whoever this bloody murderer is. Now go home." He turned and stepped through the door, slamming it behind him.

"Don't worry," Poole called to Ronald as he followed the inspector to the door. "We're going to find out who's behind all this and you can get back to your life."

Ronald nodded miserably as he watched him go.

"AREN'T we going to talk to Gina Glover, sir?" Poole asked, catching up with Brock in the corridor at the back of the theatre.

"I want to see if Sheila's got anything from Jonny Turnbull's body first," Brock answered, his pace not slowing. "And anyway, she was the one who was insisting on waiting for her lawyer. So she can wait for us for a little bit. Let her stew."

Although Poole's long stride was a match for the inspector's, his thin legs lacked the power of Brock's tree-trunk-like limbs. The large shape of Brock in front of him seemed to almost fill the small corridor, and for a moment he was reminded of the scene in *Indiana Jones* when the boulder rolled towards the hero down the tunnel. Poole suddenly felt glad to be behind the advancing inspector and not in front of him.

When they emerged into the theatre, it was to see the body of Jonny Turnbull being wheeled out through the double doors at the top of the long flight of steps that ran down the middle of the seats. Sheila was still there with two crime scene colleagues. She was standing near where the body was found and was scribbling on a clipboard as they climbed up towards her.

"What have we got, Sheila?" Brock asked as they reached her.

She turned to them, her face serious. "I don't think this guy got drunk and fell."

"Go on," Brock said.

"For starters, look at these steps." She pointed down at their feet. "They're shallow and carpeted, not exactly the right combination for someone to fall a great distance and break their neck. The other thing is, if he was drunk enough to have a bad fall, he's also unlikely to have an injury like that."

"How do you mean?" Poole asked.

"Well when you're drunk, you don't react as quickly when you fall, so you don't tense up. It's why people who are drunk or asleep tend to fare better in car crashes than those who were fully alert at the time of impact."

"I'll remember to try and be asleep if I'm ever in a car crash," Poole said.

Sheila grinned at him and carried on. "The pathologist's just left but he seems to think there's very little in the way of injury other than the broken neck, which is a bit suspicious for a fall down a flight of stairs. The only thing we've really got to go on forensics-wise is the bottle of booze. I've had a quick dust for prints, but it looks like there are only the victim's on there. I'll get it back to the lab and see if I can pull any DNA off it."

"OK, thanks, Sheila." Brock's voice was deflated. He had been expecting more. "Come on then, let's go and see Miss Glover," he said to Poole, looking at his watch. "It's getting late and we'll need to set up uniform to cover the night shift before we go back to the station and interview her. I want people stationed at the door of every room that's involved in this thing. No one else is going to die here."

"Yes, sir," Poole said promptly. He had now seen enough of these moods from the inspector to recognise what to do in the situation, and that was to be efficient and comply. When Brock was frustrated, he was liable to bite your head off with one single wrong word uttered. That type of incident always meant that a few minutes later the inspector was feeling guilty and embarrassed, and Poole was feeling slightly annoyed and hurt.

CHAPTER SEVENTEEN

Poole knocked on the door of the room and stepped back slightly so he was alongside Brock, who was tossing another boiled sweet into his mouth.

"How's the no smoking going, sir?" Poole asked.

"Let's just say I'm getting through the boiled sweets," Brock answered with a growl.

After a few moments, the door opened to reveal Gina Glover wearing a hotel bathrobe that, despite being tied around her waist, was open at the front down to her navel. Poole stared at a spot a few inches above her head with a fierce determination.

"Miss Glover," Brock asked, unfazed by the state of her dress. "We need to ask you a few more questions."

She sighed as she wound a towel around her long

red hair until it was fixed in a turban shape and stepped aside.

"It seems that that is all you're good for, Inspector: talking and talking while we're all dropping like flies around you," she said as they stepped inside, and she closed the door behind them.

A woman reclined at one end of one of the two matching sofas and nodded at them as they came in.

"This is my lawyer," Gina said, gesturing to the woman as she took a seat next to her.

Poole noticed there was a bottle of white wine in an ice bucket on the coffee table, a half-full glass in front of each woman.

Brock and Poole seated themselves on the opposite sofa on the left, Poole pulling his notebook from his jacket and opening it, pen poised.

"Can I get you gentlemen a drink?" Gina said, sitting on the sofa opposite them and crossing her toned legs in a sweeping motion.

"No," Brock said bluntly. "Instead, you can tell us why you were arguing with Jarvis Alvarado the night before the launch."

She frowned, her smooth skin wrinkling in a slightly unnatural way that suggested botox. "I'm sure I don't know what you mean, Inspector?" she said coolly. She leaned forwards and took her wine glass.

"We have a witness who's placed you there," Brock continued.

"Look," she said, smiling. "Jarvis was an arrogant arsehole who thought he could own everybody and everything. I think you'd be harder pressed to find someone who hadn't been arguing with him before he died."

"But in this instance, you were arguing about Isabella Lennon, isn't that right?"

A wave of something like shock passed across her face, but it was so fleeting it was almost indiscernible.

"And now Mr Turnbull has died as well, and you were placed near the scene of his death," Brock continued. "It seems to us as though you are right in the middle of all this, Miss Glover, and I think, for your own good, it's time you started to give us an explanation that doesn't end with you in jail for murder."

She straightened her back and stared back at the inspector. For a moment Poole thought she might throw the remaining contents of wine at him, but instead, she drained the glass and reached for the bottle to refill it.

"If you're expecting me to confess, Inspector, you're going to be disappointed," she said, leaning back with her glass now full. "I didn't do it, you see? And if you're waiting for some big revelation or clue to finding out what the hell is going on here then I don't think you're going to get that from me either."

"So, what were you arguing about?" Brock repeated.

She sighed, rolling her eyes. "As soon as we all got wind of the fact that Jarvis was influential in choosing the cast for the film version of *Foul Murder*, we all turned on each other like snakes in a sack. We all wanted to be part of it, but of course Jarvis was lording his power over us all and being a complete idiot about it all."

"And what does this have to do with Isabella Lennon?"

"Well it doesn't take a great detective such as yourself to know they were screwing each other, does it?" Gina said, smiling.

"So, you were jealous?" Brock asked, causing Gina and her lawyer to erupt in laughter.

"Jarvis really wasn't my type, Inspector," she said with a smirk.

Poole thought back to what Ronald had told them Jarvis said—something about swapping to the other team. Then he glanced down at the two wine glasses and the relaxed nature of Gina's lawyer in her company, even in an official capacity. He glanced at Brock, but could tell by his expression he had already made the same connection.

"There was something going on between Isabella and Jarvis," Gina continued, "but I have no idea if it was serious. Knowing Jarvis, it wasn't to him," she said, pausing to have another sip of wine. "I was hunting down Jarvis to try and sweet-talk him into giving me a part when I heard him talking to Isabella in the courtyard. She was telling him how she would be perfect for the role, and that they could become the next darling couple of the nation. I don't think she was offering this as a real relationship, mind you. It sounded more like a business deal to me."

She stared at her glass, seemingly lost in the recollection for a moment before looking back up at them with a shrug. "When Isabella went inside I gave Jarvis what for, told him he was being an idiot who needed to start thinking with his head rather than his pants." She shrugged as though this was the end of her offering.

Brock took a deep breath next to Poole and leaned back slightly.

"So, do you think Jarvis was going to give Isabella Lennon a part?"

"Who knows? Like I said, Jarvis would say anything to anybody to get what he wanted."

There was a silence as Gina sipped her wine thoughtfully. It was broken by Brock suddenly rising and heading for the door.

"That will be all, for now, Miss Glover. Please don't leave your room until morning."

"Wouldn't dream of it," she said, turning to her lawyer and smiling.

Poole closed the door behind them. "Blimey, sir, do you think she charges overtime for that?"

"I hope not, Poole," Brock said, grinning. "Lawyers are bloody expensive as it is."

A noise of clattering metal came from down the corridor as Jane Marx appeared around the corner with a stepladder over her shoulder and a toolbox.

Brock frowned and made his way over to her as she set the ladder down in the middle of the corridor.

"What's going on, Miss Marx?" Brock asked.

"I'm just looking at the air conditioning for Michael," she answered as she climbed the steps with a screwdriver. "Apparently this vent's not working properly."

"And you can do that, can you?" Brock asked, looking impressed.

"You learn to do all sorts in the theatre." She grinned. She began to unscrew the white metal plate that covered the air vent.

"This is a side job then, is it? Doing odd jobs at the hotel?"

"Ha! I wish. Then I might actually get paid extra for it. No, Terry lets his brother use me for jobs here and there when Dave's not around—he's the hotel's caretaker. He's getting on a bit now, so he's cut down his hours. Terry sort of loans me to his brother."

"How long have you worked here?" Poole asked.

"Oh, years now. I started at the theatre before I'd left school, dreaming of becoming an actress..." She pulled the last of the screws out and grabbed the metal sheet as it fell. "Do me a favour and lean that against the wall, will you?" she said, handing the piece to Poole. He leaned it against the corridor and looked at his watch.

"Sir, I'm going to have to go."

Brock nodded at him. "Good luck, and you know you can call me if you need me, right?"

"Yes, sir," Poole answered and turned down the corridor, trying not to panic. This was it—he was going to meet his dad.

CHAPTER EIGHTEEN

Poole ordered another large glass of red wine and stared at the door nervously. At any moment his father would walk through it and sit at his table, and the thought was making him want to leap up and run down the street as fast as he could go.

The wine bar was new but had been designed to look old and rustic. The furniture was all large, solid and made from rough, unfinished wood. Metallic, factory-style lamps hung from the ceiling and it almost had the feel of a wine cellar. Not that Poole had ever been in a wine cellar, but he imagined it would be very much like this.

Something caught his eye across the street and he saw Inspector Brock standing with his wife, Laura.

Both of them stared down at a small brown puppy that was cocking its leg against a lamp-post.

What on earth is he doing here? Poole thought, but he knew the answer before he'd even finished the thought.

The inspector was here to look out for him. He watched Brock pick up the puppy and head into the fish restaurant opposite, glancing across the street before he ducked through the door.

For a split second, Poole felt as though their eyes met across the street and through the glass. Then it was over, and the door of the wine bar was opening, framing his father against the streetlight behind.

Poole felt his stomach lurch as his right hand gripped the wine glass ever harder.

His dad's deep brown eyes scanned the room until they landed on him, his face changing into a broad smile. As he made his way through the tables and benches towards him, Poole noticed he had a slight limp. He wondered if this was something he had gained in prison, or just through the fact he was now getting older.

"You came," he said when he reached Poole's table. His voice was deep and thick with emotion, his eyes shining in the dim lighting of the wine bar.

Poole found himself already unsure of what to

say. "Drink?" he managed, lifting his wine glass slightly by way of explanation.

His father nodded and then caught a waiter's attention. He ordered something Poole had never heard of, and leaned back in his seat at ease.

"You didn't bring company this time, then?" Poole said, remembering that at his last meeting with his dad he had been flanked by heavies.

"I noticed you did," his dad said, the smile becoming harder somehow.

Poole frowned, confused, and then suddenly realised that he must mean Brock. He turned and looked out of the window and saw the back of a broad-shouldered man standing facing the restaurant opposite.

His dad hadn't come alone.

"You know," his father said, "I'm surprised they've let a puppy into a restaurant. I guess being a police inspector gives you some privileges."

Poole said nothing but took another large gulp of wine. Hearing his father talk about Brock was setting his teeth on edge.

The waiter arrived with the bottle his father had ordered. Poole watched as his father tasted it and then nodded his approval to the waiter, who filled his glass.

When he'd left, Poole spoke first.

"What do you want?" he said, trying to keep his voice even.

"I want us to have a relationship again," his dad said, his eyes fixed on him.

"You lost that right when I saw my friend die in front of me," Poole said, anger and emotion coursing through him so suddenly that he was struggling to not throw the table over and launch himself at his father.

His father nodded sadly. "I can't ever change what happened," he said, turning the wine glass slowly between his fingers. "And I know that me saying sorry won't make any difference, although I am. I just want a chance to explain what happened."

"I don't need it explained to me!" Poole said, his voice rising enough to make the others in the bar look towards their table. "I know what bloody happened. People came to our house and shot at us."

As Poole spoke, the images of that day seemed to flash in his mind like scenes from a horror film.

He had been playing with his friends on his fifteenth birthday when the first shots had fired. He had seen his friend killed and had taken a bullet in his own leg.

"It wasn't my fault, Guy," his father said. "The men who came to our house were nothing to do with my business."

Poole gave a humourless laugh and shook his head in disbelief.

"You are unbelievable."

"I don't expect you to just believe me," his dad said, leaning back and taking another draught of wine. "But I'm working on that."

Poole eyed him suspiciously. "What's that supposed to mean?"

"It means that I'm going to prove to you that what happened wasn't my fault. It won't excuse the fact that I wasn't there for you. I was sent away for decisions I had made, whether I knew I was making them or not." Poole noticed a change in his father's expression. There was not just sadness there, but a bitter anger too.

"Maybe in time you'll see me differently," Jack said, looking up at him, "and then maybe we can start over."

"Start over?" Poole said incredulously. "You're bloody deluded." He got up, his chair scraping noisily across the slate-tiled floor. "You stay away from me and Mum. We don't want anything to do with you." He turned and moved towards the door.

"How is your mum?" Jack called over his shoulder.

Poole paused, his hand on the handle of the door.

"She's better off without you," he said and stepped out into the night.

He looked at the large man who was still standing by the window. The man nodded at him in a professional manner that made Poole feel sick—as though he had just been addressed as the boss's son.

As though he was part of all this.

He marched off across the street, just wanting to put some distance between himself and his dad, when the door if the restaurant opposite opened and Laura Brock's face appeared.

"You better come in here before you go home or he's never going to be able to sleep," she said, smiling.

CHAPTER NINETEEN

Poole finished the fresh wine that had been put in front of him in record time. Despite him now being seated at a window table of the fish restaurant across the road, the wine seemed better than in the wine bar.

"He's very..." He paused trying to think of the words. "Cute," he settled on.

The Brocks' new puppy was currently curled in a ball on Poole's lap, fast asleep.

"What type is he?"

"He's a cross-breed," Laura answered. "His dad was a Border Collie and his mum was a working Cocker Spaniel."

"When she says 'cross-breed'," Brock joined in from across the table, "she means he's a mongrel."

"Sam!" Laura said, her tone sharp. "He has feelings, you know."

"Yes, but luckily he can't understand a word I say. At least he never bloody listens to commands," Brock grumbled.

"Oh, come on, Sam," Laura said, rolling her eyes. "He's just a pup."

"Anyway," Brock continued. "There's nothing wrong with being a mongrel; they're tougher than other dogs. They get far fewer health problems than pedigrees."

Laura looked at him with surprise, and then accepted this information. "Right," she said with a firm nod.

"So, come on," Brock said. He leaned forwards, placing his large elbows on the table, and stared at Poole. "What happened?"

Poole looked down at the little dog and gave it a gentle stroke. "He said it wasn't his fault."

"Not very original, is it?" Brock said.

Poole looked up at him and laughed. Somehow the tension poured out at him as Brock smiled back at him, clearly pleased to have made him laugh.

"Oh, Sam," Laura said, slapping him on his arm.

"No, you're right," Poole said. "It's not very original. He didn't even give me an explanation; he just said he was going to bring me proof that would convince me."

"Proof?" Brock said, frowning.

"That's what he said," Poole said with a shrug. "I don't see what it could be. We all know he was helping to move drugs around; that's what brought those people to our house." His voice had become thick with emotion as he reached the end of the sentence, and his arm moved away from the puppy on his lap and back to his wine glass.

Brock said nothing but watched him carefully, his large eyebrows knotted in thought.

"At least it sounds like he doesn't mean you or your mum any harm," Laura said, her hand reaching out and giving Poole's arm a squeeze.

"He's going to put us in harm's way just by being here," Poole said in a hollow voice. "He's still part of that world, which means at some point somewhere he's going to annoy the wrong people and it will come back on us. He even had some goon standing outside the café tonight while we talked."

"Well, you had me, to be fair," Brock said, smiling. "I might qualify as a goon." He smiled. "Seriously though, do you think your dad has started up his old business here?"

"Who knows, but I for one would be happy if he was back inside."

Indy raised his head from Poole's lap and let out a long, high-pitched yawn.

Almost immediately a waiter arrived at their table with a concerned smile.

"Sir, we did agree that when the animal woke up?" The waiter hovered nervously.

"Blimey," Brock said gruffly. "You didn't waste much time, did you? The little bugger's only just opened his eyes!"

"I'm sorry, sir, but we do have people eating here." The waiter gave another smile.

"All right, all right," Brock said, standing. "Come on, then." The three of them got up and Poole passed Indy to Laura. She clipped the small puppy lead on the dog and placed him on the tiled floor.

"I'm taking this," Brock said, scooping the wine bottle from the table as they headed towards the door.

Poole's eyes strayed towards the wine bar across the street, but he knew his father had long gone. He had watched him and the large companion leave through the window a while ago. Still, he couldn't shake the feeling that his father would appear at any moment. He wondered if he would always feel like this now that Jack Poole was out and living in the area.

"No!" cried Laura suddenly from behind him.

He turned to see Indy squatting on the internal doormat. Laura reached down, grabbed the dog and lifted him forwards onto the street, but there was already a small, dark puddle on the doormat.

The waiter glared as he closed the door while the three of them burst into laughter.

"WHAT HAPPENED?" Jenny Poole said, leaping to her feet as soon as Guy had stepped through the door.

"It's fine, Mum," Poole said, alarmed at her panic. He hung his coat on the line of pegs to the left of the door and moved across to her.

She squeezed him in a tight embrace, as though to make sure he was really there. The faint scent of cannabis reached his nostrils, but he decided to ignore it for today.

"What did the bastard have to say?" his mum said, pulling away from him, her face suddenly full of anger.

"He said that it wasn't his fault," Poole said. He watched her face move from anger to a shocked incredulity and then back again.

"He's got some nerve coming here and arranging these secret meetings with you just to say it's not his fault!" she shouted. Poole could see her trembling and moved to the kitchen to fetch them both a glass of wine. "The least he could do is own his mistakes and apologise."

"He did apologise," Poole said without thinking.

"Oh, so that makes it all all right, does it?" she shrieked, her anger turning on him.

"No, Mum," Poole said softly, walking back to her and handing her the wine. "Nothing can make it all right."

She nodded, and physically sagged, as though a furious wind had suddenly been knocked out of her. A single, fat tear rolled down her cheek and Guy put one long arm around her and pulled her to his chest.

"COME ON, THEN," Laura said as they stepped into the hallway of their semi-detached house. "What's bothering you?"

"What do you mean?" Brock said, kicking off his shoes as Indy excitedly scrabbled along the wooden floor of the hallway towards the kitchen.

"You've barely said a word since we left Guy, and I know that look," she said, turning to him. "It's the look you get when something's worrying you but you're too stubborn to talk about it. Then you gradually get grumpier and grumpier until I want to smack you one, so shall we skip all that and just get to the problem?"

He was still scowling, but the way she had so clearly laid out this particular personality flaw had him trying not to smile.

"All right," he said, sighing as he moved past her into the kitchen. "If you really want to know, it's this situation with Poole's father."

"Obviously," Laura said in a sarcastic tone. "But what is it? Do you think he's dangerous?"

"I think that the last time he was in Poole's life, Guy ended up taking a bullet to the leg and seeing his friend die, so yes, I think he's dangerous."

"But didn't you say you encouraged him to go and meet him?" Laura said, leaning on the kitchen island worktop and looking across at him as he leaned back on the counter opposite her.

"Yes, because I could see he needed to. The man is still his father. He needs to put this to bed so he can move on from it, but it doesn't mean I like it."

Laura turned and scooped up Indy, who had been pawing at her leg. They fell into silence for a moment. Brock studied her face, feeling awkward. For some reason, any mention of parenthood seemed to have this effect on them these days, paralysing them into silence, neither of them wanting to vocalise the topic that constantly hovered in their home, the lack of children making the silence of the empty house louder and louder by the day.

"I'm sorry," Brock said, breaking the silence. "I'm probably just worrying over nothing. It's just..." He paused and looked down at his feet.

"You still think you're the cursed detective?" Laura said softly.

He looked up at her and nodded with a weak smile. She moved to the counter and leaned into him as his thick arm encircled her.

Indy nuzzled in happily between them.

CHAPTER TWENTY

"So, how's it going in the world of celebrity?" Anderson sneered at Poole as he came alongside him at the coffee machine in Bexford Station canteen.

"Fine, thank you," Poole said, wishing the machine was faster. Its low gurgling and grinding seemed to take forever before a small stream of dark brown liquid began hitting the mug below.

"Oh, really?" Anderson said. "That's not what I've heard. I heard you've got some maniac piling bodies up while you're sitting around chatting to the stars."

"And have you caught whoever killed that woman?" Poole said, looking back at him. "Or are you too busy wasting time gossiping about other cases?"

"We'll get them," Anderson said. He seemed rattled by Poole bringing up the case. Poole guessed it wasn't going well.

"Still no leads then, eh?" Poole said as he pulled one finished mug from under the coffee machine and placed the second one under it.

"Why don't you just worry about your celebrities?" Anderson muttered darkly.

Poole took the second cup and headed back to the table where Brock was waiting, having just finished his breakfast.

When they had arrived, the inspector had begun to order a large fried breakfast when he had hesitated, looked at Poole, and then ordered a single slice of toast and marmalade. He had been in a mood ever since.

"And what did the boy wonder over there want?" Block said, staring at the back of Anderson's head so fiercely that even from across the room Poole was surprised to see it not smoking.

"He wanted to congratulate us on the progress of our case," Poole said, sitting down and sliding one mug of coffee across to Brock.

"Ha, I bet he did. How are he and Sharp getting on with their case?"

"Not well, by the sounds of it," Poole answered, taking a sip of the steaming drink in front of him and looking back at the file laid out before him. "Strange, there being two murders within a few days of each other."

"Yes," Brock said slowly.

Poole looked up at him. The inspector's grey eyes were glazed over as he stared sightlessly towards the ceiling.

"Sir?" he said questioningly, causing Brock to snap back to him.

"Might be worth me having a chat with Sharp later, just to make sure there's nothing related between the cases."

"Yes, sir," Poole replied dutifully, despite not being able to see any connection between the cases from what he'd heard.

"So," Brock said, turning back to the file in front of them. "There isn't much here for us?"

He gestured to the reports on Jonny Turnbull's death from both the pathologist and the crime scene team.

"Not really," Poole answered, flicking through the sheets. "It looks like the pathologist agrees with Sheila. It seems as though it would be pretty unlikely for Turnbull to have broken his neck like that on those stairs."

Brock grunted but said nothing, which Poole took as a sign to continue.

"Sheila got nothing from the bottle that Jonny Turnbull had, only his prints on it."

"Hold on a minute—only his prints?" Brock said, frowning.

"Yes, sir."

"If he had bought it in the hotel you'd expect the barman's fingers to be on it, wouldn't you?"

"Good point," Poole said, thinking.

"Hold on, though. The killer can't have cleaned it afterwards because Turnbull's prints were still on it, which means either Turnbull bought it and wiped it clean of prints before adding his own, which doesn't make sense, or the killer got the whiskey for him and wiped their prints off first."

A smile flickered through Brock's stormy expression like lightning, and was gone just as quickly

"Exactly," he said. "So we need to find where bottle was bought. Someone might even remember a person buying that brand and wearing gloves."

"That'll be tricky, sir," Poole said doubtfully. He was thinking of every shop, pub and bar in Addervale where the bottle could have been bought and concluding that it was pretty much impossible.

"Maybe, but my guess is it would have been bought nearby, so we'll start there and work out." Brock looked down at the sheet in front of him. "And the time of death for Jonny Turnbull looks to have been around ten o'clock. Let's check the footage again from the cameras at the hotel." He shook his head. "I can't believe they only have cameras at the entrance to the place, and then the entrance to the car park. How could they not have one in the car park itself with all those fancy cars in there?"

"They do actually, sir," Poole said distractedly as he continued to read.

"What do you mean?"

Poole looked up. "Well there is a camera in there, but it's been broken for a week or so. Apparently, they haven't got around to fixing it with all the preparations for the *Foul Murder* cast coming to stay."

Poole watched Brock's face, trying to read it, but it was as expressionless as stone until he drained the last of his coffee and got up.

"Come on, let's get back down there and try and get to the bottom of this mess."

Poole dropped their cup back on the counter as he moved towards the door where Constable Davies, appeared holding a newspaper.

"Sir!" His face was lit up with a nervous excitement. "You've got to see this!"

He turned it around and showed them the headline in bright red letters.

PATRICK PROFITS FROM CAST CARNAGE

IN THE TOP left-hand corner of the page was a picture of Eli Patrick, deliberately taken and manipulated to make him look sinister.

CHAPTER TWENTY-ONE

"So, Mr Patrick," Brock said, his elbows resting on his knees and his hands together. "It seems as though you have got your big break?"

They were sitting in Eli's room in the Sinton Hotel across from the young actor who was wearing a bright blue jumper and cream chinos.

"Oh, it's just paper talk," Eli said, shifting awkwardly in his chair.

Brock picked up the newspaper he had thrown onto the coffee table between them. He lifted it and began to read from page four, which it was already turned to.

"'With the tragic events which have unfolded in the small, picturesque city of Bexford over the last few days, it appears there is an unlikely winner. Young newbie to the *Foul Murder* cast, Eli Patrick, is said to now be in discussion with Paramour Pictures about taking the lead in the upcoming big-screen version of the hit TV crime drama.'"

Brock threw the paperback own on the table and looked back at Eli, who was biting his top lip.

"So, as the paper says, this has all worked out pretty well for you, hasn't it, Mr Patrick?"

"Look," Eli said, one hand flopping back his golden hair. "I want to be honest with you chaps. *Foul Murder*, the TV show, is my big break. Pretty sure it's the only one I'm ever going to get."

"Why do you say that?" Poole asked.

"Because I can't bloody act!" the young man said, laughing. "I can't remember my lines, I'm always accidentally looking at something behind the camera halfway through a scene—I'm bloody useless at it!"

"Excuse my ignorance, Mr Patrick, but if you're so bad, how did you get on one of the most popular shows in the country?" Brock asked.

"My mum is a failed actress, and all my life she's been trying to get me to fulfil her dreams. My uncle works at the TV station and she forced him to get me a part." He gave them a sheepish smile. "Truth be told, I'm not very good at anything. I'm one of those born loafer types."

"And yet here you are," Brock said, "about to

profit from the death of two men who you had the means and motive to murder."

"Now come on," Eli said pleadingly. "You can't really think I had anything to do with all this?"

"Where were you at ten o'clock last night?"

"Is that when Jonny died?"

"Yes. Can you answer the question please?"

"Oh," Eli said, jumping upright in his seat. "I've got an alibi!"

"Let's hear it then," Brock barked.

"I was with Jane last night in this very room!" Eli said triumphantly.

"Jane?"

"Yes, Jane Marx. You know, the girl who works in the theatre."

"And how long has this relationship been going on?" Brock asked, the tone of his voice indicating to Poole that he saw this as another suspect to tick off the list.

"Oh, not really a relationship, just a casual thing really. Likes actors." He grinned at them, relaxed now that he was sure he was off the hook.

"And did she stay the night with you?"

"Yes, she left first thing. I'd had a bit too much whiskey I'm afraid, so I slept in."

Brock nodded and rose as Poole finished up the

last of his notes and joined him heading towards the door.

"We still don't want you going anywhere, Mr Patrick," Brock said over his shoulder.

"Wouldn't dream of it," Eli replied. "Sitting around and passing the time with food and drink is pretty much my aim in life."

AS THEY DESCENDED the large staircase from Eli Patrick's room, they saw the sashaying figure of Gina Glover heading towards them, a pleading Mike Hart in tow.

"But Gina, be reasonable. Think of all I've done for you here!" he said, trying to keep up with her determined pace.

She stopped and turned to him, the red hem of her wide dress swooping out around her.

"All you've done for me!" she said, venom dripping from every word. "Do you mean when you were sucking up to Isabella because you thought she might be given a role as Jarvis' little plaything? Or when you told me that I wasn't right for the part?"

"That was a different part!" Mike Hart cried, throwing his hands up in the air. "That was when I thought we were talking about a bit part! I think you're perfect for this! You'll own this film, I know you will."

Gina turned away from him with a loud huff and started back up the stairs when she caught sight of Brock and Poole.

"Miss Glover, can I ask what all this is about?" Brock said, taking the last few steps towards her.

"Well, Inspector, here's a little insight into how this industry operates," Gina said, putting her hands on her hips and half turning to Mike Hart. "Little worms like Mike here won't do a thing for you—won't put in a good word anywhere, won't make sure your role on the show has decent storylines other than just wearing a tight dress, nothing. Then when you finally get a break from somewhere else, they come crawling to you, telling you how much they've done for you. Isn't that right, Mike?"

Hart shook his head with a smile. "Gina, just take some time and think it over. You're going to need someone you can trust alongside you in this."

"Ha!" Gina said, her eyes rolling. "Now he thinks he's someone I can trust!" She spun her attention back to Brock and Poole. "I think you should ask Mike here why I saw him taking a load of sheets from Jarvis' room a couple of nights before he died."

Hart's head snapped to her and then back to the inspector.

"Sheets?" Brock said slowly, staring at him.

"I know!" Gina said. "I mean, I dread to think what Jarvis might have been up to; he always was a filthy sod."

Mike Hart shifted nervously. "Can we talk somewhere else?"

"Please do," Gina said. "I don't want to hear the sordid details." She marched past them and headed up the stairs.

"Come on," Brock said, as he headed downward.

"Actually," Mike Hart said, his face paling. "I don't think I should say anything further until I speak to my lawyer."

Brock stopped and turned back to him before glancing at Poole.

"Are you getting a sense of déjà vu as well?"

"Not unless Mr Hart's lawyer wants to sleep with him, sir." Poole grinned.

Mike Hart looked at them both as though they were mad.

"Well, you heard the man, Poole," Brock said. "I think we should carry on this chat back at the station. At least Mr Hart here won't be bringing press attention on us."

CHAPTER TWENTY-TWO

Poole stepped back into the interview room and placed two glasses of water in front of Mike Hart and his lawyer before taking his seat next to Brock.

Hart had stuck to his word and not spoken since they had left the hotel. Thankfully his lawyer had arrived with surprising speed, and after a private consultation with him, the producer was now ready to talk.

"Jarvis was a sex addict, OK?" Hart said.

Poole glanced at the lawyer and saw his face was as expressionless as stone.

"He was a nightmare—always at the extras, disappearing from the set all the bloody time with one of them. We were always making excuses for him, saying that we needed to run some set repairs or something."

"OK, so what does this have to do with what happened with the sheets?" Brock said.

Hart hung his head and shook it at the floor. "Look, I didn't know at the time what it was about, and it might be nothing now, but..."

"Just tell us what happened, Mr Hart," Brock said.

"The morning before the launch event, Jarvis called me and asked me to go to his room. It was maybe eleven o'clock? So, I went, and when he opens the door he looks up and down the corridor, shoves a load of bed sheets in my hands, tells me to get rid of them and get the hotel to give him some new ones."

"And you didn't think there was anything suspicious in this?" Poole said, slightly incredulous at the idea.

"You don't know show business, do you?" Hart said with a chuckle. "Everyone's half mad and believe me, there are weirder things than that happening every day."

"And did he give you a reason for wanting to get rid of these sheets?" Brock said.

"No. I asked him if everything was all right, but he said it was fine and shut the door on me."

"And how did he seem when you spoke to him?"

"A bit rattled, nervy for him. He was always a cocky bloke, never let anything bother him, but that night he seemed a bit spooked."

"And what did you do with the bedding?"

"I threw it in the bins at the back of the hotel."

Brock turned to Constable Sanita Sanders, who was standing in the corner of the room. He nodded at her and she nodded back, a silent understanding passing between them. She left the room and Brock turned back to Hart.

"And did you get new bedding for Mr Alvarado?"

"Yes, I went to reception and got them to give it to me directly. I took it up to him that night."

"And?" Poole asked impatiently.

"And nothing. He took them and shut the door in my face again."

"Did you talk about it the next day?"

"No. The next day Jarvis was back to his normal self, winding everyone up and being the big star," he said, somewhat bitterly.

"You'd better hope we find those sheets, Mr Hart," Brock said gruffly as he got up and headed for the door.

Poole got up to follow him as his phone began to buzz in his pocket.

He pulled the phone from his pocket as he

stepped out into the corridor, glancing at the unknown number on the screen.

"Hello?" he said as he continued after Brock.

"Hello, Guy. It's your dad."

Poole stopped dead in his tracks, that familiar ice running through his veins. "How did you get my number?"

"I've got something I thought might help you," his father said down the line.

"Help me?" Poole said, his head spinning. He looked up at the Brock, who was almost at the other end of the corridor now and heading towards the door at the end.

"That girl that was killed earlier in the week."

Poole frowned, for a moment thinking only of the deaths of Jarvis Alvarado and Jonny Turnbull. Then he remembered Ella Louise, the girl in Anderson and Sharp's case.

"What about her?" Poole said, unable to keep the sense of dread from his voice. Had his father had something to do with the girl's death? The thought was too much to take.

"She was an escort for a bloke called Ian Ganning."

Poole frowned, confused. He was pretty sure that Sharp and Anderson would know this. "And?"

"Well from what I've heard, Ian has told your lot

that this girl wasn't working for him that night."

Poole heard voices in the background on the other end of the line. The line was muffled for a moment, as though his father had placed his hand over the phone. Either his dad didn't know where the mute button was, or this was a landline. Poole pulled the phone from his ear and looked at the number again. It had a Bexford code. He made a mental note to look up the address after the call. He placed the phone back to his ear as his father's voice returned.

"Look, I've got to go. All I know is she was working that night. Don't ask me how, and if you try and bring me in for a statement I'll deny all knowledge of it. Speak to you later, son."

The line went dead. Poole's mind raced. Movement ahead of him made him look up into the face of Constable Sanders.

"Are you OK?" she said, pausing as she saw him. "Sir," she added quickly, remembering where she was.

"Yes, fine," he said, marching off, his long stride eating up the cheap, tiled carpet of the corridor as Sanita watched him with confusion and a small amount of hurt in her eyes.

Poole marched on, straight through to the main office, pausing as he caught sight of Anderson across the room.

No. He needed to talk to Brock first.

Anderson had noticed him staring and was now looking at him with a mixture of curiosity and annoyance. Poole turned away and headed towards the canteen. Pushing through the double doors, he saw Brock at the coffee machine and moved alongside him.

"Sir," he said his voice in a low whisper. "I need to talk to you in the office."

Brock looked at him, his thick eyebrows dotted in a frown. He grunted an agreement and, after scooping his coffee up, turned back towards the door with Poole in tow.

Neither of them spoke until they had reached the small office that they shared.

"What's happened?" Brock asked as he closed the door, his tone hard and urgent.

"My dad called me and gave me information on Inspector Sharp's case," Poole said bluntly.

Brock slumped into his chair and sighed. "Go on."

Poole filled him in, trying to read the inspector's reaction to the news as he did so. Brock calmly sipped his coffee and stared down at his desk until Poole fell silent.

"I need to tell Inspector Sharp, sir," Poole said.

"Of course you do," Brock answered. "But I'm not sure you want to reveal the source."

"I don't really, sir, no."

Brock nodded. "Wait here." He jumped up and left the room in a matter of seconds. Poole turned to his computer and pulled his phone from his pocket. By the time the inspector had returned, Poole had noted an address gathered from the number and carefully folded it into his pocket.

"Sharp's got the info," Brock said. He had seen Poole slip the paper into his pocket but said nothing about it.

"What did you tell him?" Poole asked.

"I told him it had come from an informant, but that he'd need to check it out for himself." He looked at Poole as though deciding something. After what felt like an age, he spoke.

"Be careful here, Poole. I don't know how your dad knew what he knew, but using information like this in a case is risky. Let's not make a habit of it, OK?"

His tone was so serious that Poole had replied with a clipped, "Yes, sir," before he had even realised it.

"Now let's get down to the hotel," Brock said. "I can't get Davies on his mobile and I need him to go and look for those sheets."

CHAPTER TWENTY-THREE

"What the bloody hell is all this?!" Brock grumbled as Poole guided the car towards the Sinton Hotel.

Outside a small crowd were gathered, the cameras and microphones held by many of them making it clear they were journalists.

"I thought all this lot had buggered off," Brock said as they passed the crowd, turning in through the archway to the small courtyard at the rear of the hotel.

They stepped out and headed through the back door and into the lobby, which was full of people. A group of men and women in expensive-looking suits loitered to their left, while the rest of the room was filled with young, good-looking people who were laughing and joking loudly. This party atmosphere was accentuated by the fact that everyone in the room held a flute of champagne as waiters and waitresses buzzed about with silver trays full of canapés.

Brock accosted a waiter who had a selection of small curls of raw beef, each with a dollop of horseradish.

"What's all this about?" he asked the man, as he helped himself to two of the rolls.

"It's the announcement of the new *Foul Murder* film," the waiter asked with an amused expression. "Have you gate-crashed or something? The normal hotel guests aren't allowed in here for this."

"Well, it's a good thing we're not normal guests then, isn't it?" Brock said, taking another slice of beef and stepping past him into the crowd.

Poole followed, looking up as the main doors opened and the press began to flood in. He noticed Mike Hart was the person responsible for opening the doors and pointed him out to Brock, who headed towards him like a large shark parting the waves.

"What the bloody hell is going on?" Brock said as they reached Hart, still sporting the black polo-necked shirt he always seemed to wear, now paired with a suit jacket.

"They're announcing the film," he answered miserably.

"Now?!" Brock thundered over the dull humour of the room. "When there have just been two murders here?"

"No better time." Hart shrugged. "The publicity's through the roof. They've got a box office hit on their hands before they've even made the thing."

Brock snatched a flute of champagne and some small pastries from two passing waiters and shook his head. "Some people will try and exploit any situation."

"And where are the rest of the cast?" Poole asked.

Mike Hart looked at him nervously. "Gina will be making her grand entrance in a moment. She's going to be confirmed as the lead in the film. Eli's somewhere around here. I saw him talking to some of the film people a while ago with Jane Marx from the theatre." He turned his eyes to the crowd and began scanning it.

"And what about Miss Lennon?" Poole asked.

"Isabella's gone back to London," Hart said meekly.

"What?!" Brock said, spinning back to him and spraying pastry for his mouth.

"Look, it's not my fault," Hart said, stepping back from the reddening Brock. "Ask your constable over there; he's the one who had the fight with her."

Brock followed his finger and looked across the room to where Constable Davies was standing behind the reception desk, talking to a middle-aged woman.

Brock set off, marching across the room and parting the crowd like a professional rugby player.

"Davies," Brock roared as he arrived at the desk. "Why the bloody hell has one of my murder suspects been allowed to leave?"

Davies turned to him, righting his helmet as it slipped on his head. Now that he was looking at them, they could see the forming of a black eye on the left side of his face.

"I'm sorry, sir. I told her she couldn't go and she hit me with her handbag," Davies said in a weak voice. "I think she had a bowling ball in it," he added darkly.

"And what exactly did you do then? Just let her walk out of here?"

"I was knocked out for a little bit, sir," Davies said, his cheeks reddening. "But we're checking the footage of the outside camera to see if we can get a look at the car she left in."

Poole watched Brock's face change from one of annoyance to something calmer.

"OK, Davies, good work. When you've done that I want you to get out the back and check the large wheelie bins there for any bed sheets you can find."

"Bed sheets, sir?" Davies said, looking confused.

"Bed sheets," Brock confirmed. "Then bag them up somehow and get them to the lab to see what they can pull off them. Rush job, as fast as they can."

"Yes, sir," Davies said, bewildered.

Brock turned and walked a few steps away before scanning the crowd.

"I think we need to go and talk to the people in suits," he said as Poole joined him. They moved back across the lobby to the group who looked as though they had been taking full advantage of the free alcohol.

"I'm Detective Inspector Brock, and this is Detective Sergeant Poole." Brock's loud voice cut across a young, brash-looking man who had been telling a story of some sort.

"Ah, the police!" the man said, turning to them. "I wondered when we could expect a visit from you."

"And you are?"

"Chester Lavington," the man answered. "This is my picture."

"So, it's you that's been changing your mind over the lead in the film?"

The man's smile flickered. "Hardly changing our minds, Inspector; it's more that our choices have been dropping like flies—which I think is your job to stop, unless I'm mistaken?"

A thick silence spread over the group, seeming to block out the noise of the room. Poole watched Brock's jaw tighten as he took a step forwards.

"Believe it or not, Mr Lavington," Brock said, his voice a low growl, "I've met people like you before. Little people with money that lets them act like they're above everybody else. But they're not, are they Mr Lavington?" Brock inched closer as Lavington tried to back up but found the wall behind him. "This flashy persona, the cocky manner, it's all just there in the hope that people don't see the real you and realise what a tiny little worm of a person you are."

Lavington's mouth opened and shut like a fish.

"Now, I think you should tell us who you told about the changes to the lead role of this and when you told them, and then we might be able to catch this lunatic."

"We told all of them different things," Lavington blurted out. "We were trying to play them off against each other, get them all hungry for the part so they would bad-mouth each other in the press, and we would get some publicity out of it. I can get my PA to give you the details," he stammered, his eyes pleading that this would be enough.

Brock turned and walked away abruptly, leaving the rest of the group shuffling nervously as Poole took the details of Lavington's PA and moved towards Brock, who was standing a few feet away.

"I rather think Miss Glover is about to make her entrance," Brock said, smiling as his gaze fixed on the red-headed figure of Gina who had appeared at the top of the stairs.

Poole couldn't help but notice that Brock's mood seemed to have suddenly improved greatly. He often likened the inspector to a steam pipe whose pressure needed to be released periodically or he'd blow up. He was just grateful that there were other people in the world to take some of these releases, not just him.

The press had noticed Gina now and a murmur flew around the lobby as the crowd turned towards her as one.

As she descended and the cameras flashed, Poole's phone buzzed in his pocket.

"Hello?" he said, sticking one finger in his ear to try and block out the noise of the room.

"Poole? It's Anderson."

"Anderson? What do you want?"

"It looks like our case is connected to yours."

CHAPTER TWENTY-FOUR

"Now, Sam, I want you to remember that this is still my case," Detective Inspector Roderick Sharp said, "and I'm going to pursue it as such."

He looked up at Brock, his perfectly rectangular moustache bristling either in the wind or with indignation.

Sharp and Anderson had arrived just twenty minutes later at the hotel, and Brock and Poole had stepped out to join them.

"That's fine with me, Rod, but we're dealing with two deaths here and some maniac who might not be finished. If your girl is mixed up in this somehow, I'd put money on her killer being the same as ours."

Poole glanced at Anderson, who was standing next to the much shorter figure of Sharp with his arms folded. A sneer of distaste played on his lips and he for all the world gave the impression of a man who did not want to be there.

"Just tell us what the link is," Brock said firmly.

"Apparently Ella Louise was hired through her agency on Tuesday night, the night she died, and her client was someone in this hotel."

"Who?" Brock asked urgently.

"We don't know; they never gave a name. All we know is it was a woman."

"A woman?" Brock said, one magnificent eyebrow rising to the overcast sky.

"That's right. Can you think of anyone who might have—" Sharp cleared his throat as though he was finding the conversation uncomfortable "—done that from the hotel?"

Brock's eyes narrowed. "I think we need to find Isabella Lennon."

"And who's that when she's at home?" Sharp said in his clipped, military tone.

"She was having a sexual relationship with our first victim, Jarvis Alvarado."

Sharp snorted. "Then she hardly seems the type to have been calling up an escort, does she?"

"Actually," Brock said, "I'm starting to wonder if all three of them might have had a date together."

"Good lord!" Sharp said, turning to Anderson as

though looking for confirmation that such things could indeed happen.

Anderson continued to seethe from behind Sharp, as he had done since they had arrived, staring at Poole with thinly veiled hatred.

"Poole, we need to get to Isabella Lennon," Brock said, turning and walking away.

"I want to be kept up to date with everything, Sam!" Sharp called from behind them.

"Will do, Rod!" Brock called back, smiling.

"It's Roderick!" the cry came back.

"Anderson really doesn't like you, does he?" Brock said with a chuckle, his good mood apparently continuing. "It looked like he was trying to make your head fall off by staring at you."

"I think he thinks we always get the good cases, sir," Poole answered honestly.

"Then he's an idiot," the inspector answered, his face suddenly grim. "There's nothing good about murder, no matter how famous the people being killed are."

"So, shall I go and check with Davies to see whether he's got the number of the car Isabella Lennon got into?"

"Could do," Brock answered, "but first you should get some uniform to go round to her house in London."

"You think she's gone back there?"

"I don't know yet; that's why you need to send uniform around."

Poole smiled and pulled his phone from his pocket and then paused.

"Do you think Isabella Lennon made that call, sir?"

"Think about it, Poole. Isabella Lennon was seen leaving Alvarado's room the next morning. She said herself she slept with him that night. Then he gets Mike Hart to get rid of the sheets the next day. Why would he do that?"

Poole stopped in shock. "You think Alvarado killed the escort in the hotel room?"

"Maybe. But I think it's more likely that the three of them had a little fun, and then somehow that girl was killed and he panicked about possibly having her DNA in his hotel room."

"But Isabella Lennon couldn't have killed her; she was with Alvarado until the morning when Eli Patrick saw her leave."

"You heard how much Alvarado liked a drink. He could have been snoring his head off with Isabella sneaking out to kill this Ella Louise."

"Why would she though, sir?"

Brock shrugged. "Jealousy? Maybe Isabella

wasn't a fan of Ella Louise getting involved and Jarvis forced her? Maybe she took it out on her?"

"Bloody hell."

The phone hung limply by his side as he stared into space.

"The phone, Poole?" Brock said, waking him from his thoughts.

"Oh, yes," Poole said, raising it and beginning to dial. "Hold on though, sir," he said, lowering it again. "There's someone else who could have made that call. Gina Glover."

Brock nodded. "She could have, but I don't see why she'd then want to kill the woman afterwards. Unless someone else did it and the two cases being connected is just a coincidence. Let's start with finding Isabella Lennon. She's the one who's run off, after all."

"MY CLIENT CANNOT BE KEPT a virtual prisoner in some dusty old hotel indefinitely!" said Isabella Lennon's lawyer, a thin man whose head appeared to have grown up out of his hair like a small mountain.

"So, you'd like us to just let Miss Lennon here go

about her business while we know she's been lying in a murder enquiry, do you?"

The man looked towards his client, who had suddenly looked up from picking at a hangnail.

"And what is it I'm supposed to have lied about?" she said in a mildly amused tone.

"On the night before Jarvis Alvarado was murdered, you spent the night with him in his hotel room, is that correct?"

She shrugged in a bored manner. "So?"

"Who else was there?" The inspector's voice was suddenly quiet, and all the more menacing for it.

"What do you mean who else was there?" Isabella replied, looking confused.

"I mean, Miss Lennon, who else was there in the room with you and Jarvis Alvarado the night before he died?"

"No one else was bloody there. What on earth are you talking about?" she said, sitting up, her eyes narrowing in anger.

"I'm talking about Ella Louise," Brock said flatly.

"Don't say another word," Isabella's lawyer cut in as she began to reply. "I need to confer with my client in private."

"I bet you do," Brock said, standing and walking from the room.

"Sir!" Davies called to them as they stepped

outside of the room. They watched his wild, gangly run come to an untidy halt, which caused his helmet to slide down over his eyes. He pushed it back and looked at them, excitedly.

Brock and Poole both immediately recoiled at the sight and smell of Davies, who appeared to have been dipped in something gooey and then rolled in litter.

"We've found the sheets, sir!"

"Good. What sort of state are they in?"

"Well there were loads of bins, sir. I had to go through three before I found it!"

Davies was beaming with pride.

"Excellent work, Davies," Brock said, making Davies' grin spread even wider.

"And you've dropped it off at the lab?"

"Yes, sir, but they say it will be at least a day."

"Right. Well, I think it's best you go and have a shower, get your uniform cleaned." Brock paused. "Maybe shave your head?"

"Yes, sir!" Davies said, turning on his heels.

"That last one was a joke, Davies!" Poole called after him. Brock chuckled before his face turned grim again.

"I'd put money on the fact that Ella Louise's DNA is going to be all over those sheets. I say we use this to try and squeeze Miss Lennon in there, don't you?"

He barged back through the interview room door without knocking. Poole stepped into the room just in time to see Isabella's lawyer land back in his seat from where the inspector had made him jump.

"Right, Miss Lennon," Brock started, sitting down heavily in the right-hand chair opposite her. "I hope you've had enough time to confer about whatever it is you needed to confer about?"

She said nothing, but eyed him as though he was something she'd stepped in, her large, doll-like face showing nothing but contempt.

"You see, Miss Lennon, we've just found the sheets from Mr Alvarado's bed that he tried to dispose of." Brock let the statement hang in the air, waiting for her to digest it.

Her face switched from anger to a blank confusion. "What do you mean 'tried to dispose of'?"

"Jarvis Alvarado handed the sheets from his hotel room bed to Mike Hart to throw in the bins behind the hotel."

Isabella stared at him as though he was speaking a different language.

"Then we find out that Ella Louise was an escort and was hired that night by someone in the hotel. A woman."

"Oh my God," Isabella said, her face turning pale

despite the hours in the tanning salon. "You think I called this woman?"

"I think that when we find Ella Louise's DNA on Jarvis' sheets we'll be able to derive that she was in his room that night, and if you were too, then you were part of it. You made the call. Why did you kill her, Isabella? Was it just jealousy? Did you not know what you were getting into when Jarvis asked you to make that call?"

Isabella said nothing, her eyes wide.

"And then what happened? Did Jarvis find out what you had done the next morning? He must have realised that Ella Louise had been killed at least, because he got rid of the sheets."

"I don't know anything about this," Isabella said. All the cocky brattishness had gone from her demeanour. Her thin frame, which she normally held with an assertive grace, was pulled close. She now looked like a scared young woman.

"Then how do you explain it?" Brock asked simply.

"I don't know," she said in a small voice. "I don't know why Jarvis would get rid of the sheets, but I didn't call that woman. I didn't kill her."

CHAPTER TWENTY-FIVE

"Something's not right about this," Brock said to Poole who was sitting opposite him in the canteen, both nursing a coffee.

They had taken a break from interviewing Isabella Lennon and had been looking over the case notes from the Ella Louise murder. There wasn't much to go on. She had been found, hit over the head and then strangled with a cloth, in a side alley that was on the other side of Bexford from the hotel and theatre.

"I just don't think Isabella Lennon is that good an actress," Brock continued.

"If you'd seen the show, you'd know she wasn't," answered Poole. "But if she's telling the truth and she didn't call the escort agency, who did?"

They fell silent as they both sipped at their drinks.

"Gina Glover's the one who's benefitted the most," Poole said. "She could have called her."

"She could have called the escort for herself, but then why would Jarvis have been desperate to get rid of those sheets? Him sleeping with Ella Louise is the only thing that makes sense. I can't see Gina calling an escort for him; from what I've gathered she didn't even like him. Unless," Brock said, looking up at the ceiling, "Gina was trying to leverage Jarvis into giving her a role and this was part of her bribe? No," he said suddenly, shaking his head. "I can't see it."

"OK, so maybe it's unrelated?" Poole said. "Maybe it was some other guest at the hotel and Alvarado was getting rid of his sheets for some other reason?"

"Maybe, but it's too much of a coincidence."

Poole stared at the sheets in front of him, his eyes unseeing, when something occurred to him. He got up quickly. "Wait here a minute, sir. I won't be long."

He left Brock staring after him with his eyebrows raised and headed towards the main office, where he almost walked straight into Sanita Sanders.

"Oh, hi," he said awkwardly, remembering that the last time he had seen her he had rushed off when on the phone to his father.

"Sir," she said with a nod. They waited for a moment in silence before Poole remembered the task in hand.

"I'm sorry, but I've got to go," he said.

She nodded. "Yes, sir."

"Shall we talk later?"

"OK," she said, looking slightly confused.

Poole moved away before his mouth said anything else his brain would instantly regret.

Why on earth did he find himself so awkward around her when they were alone? He was a grown man! And why had he said they would talk later, as though there was something they needed to discuss just between them?

He closed his eyes and swore as he made his way to the back of the building and the small row of holding cells.

"Hello, sir," said a large, forlorn figure sitting behind the desk on the right before the short corridor that led to the holding cells.

"What are you doing here, Roland—I mean, Constable?" Poole asked, his head still reeling slightly from his encounter with Sanita.

"Apparently, I didn't handle the press enquiries very well on reception, so they've thrown me back here until this case is all sorted and it's quietened down."

Despite himself, Poole was curious. "What did you do?"

Roland grinned. "I kept giving them little bits of false information, sending them all over town."

Poole couldn't help but smile.

"Which cell is Isabella Lennon in?"

"Cell four," Roland answered. "The first celeb we've had I here, I think. She doesn't seem happy with it, that's for sure."

Poole headed down to the cell and slid the metal viewing plate across.

"Isabella? It's Sergeant Poole. I need to know the exact time you arrived at Jarvis' room."

"I've already told you!" Isabella said, standing up from the plastic, padded bench. "I got there around ten, I was on the phone with my agent before that and then I got a message from Jarvis."

"Right," Poole said, sliding the plate back and setting off back down the corridor.

Once back in the main office he turned right, through the door to the offices of the inspectors and knocked hard on the door of Inspector Sharp.

"Come in!" came a voice from the other side.

Poole hesitated. The voice wasn't Sharp's, as he had expected, but Anderson's.

He opened the door reluctantly.

"What do you want?" Anderson said with a

sneer.

Poole glanced at the empty chair behind the larger desk at the back of the room before turning back to Anderson.

"What time was the call made to book the escort? What time did she go? It wasn't in the case notes you gave us because you only found out afterwards."

"Why do you want to know?" Anderson said, leaning back in his chair and putting his hands behind his head, his muscular arms straining against his shirt sleeves.

Poole stared back at him but knew he needed to share what they had on the case that seemed to be now linked with Anderson's.

"We know that someone, a woman, called the escort agency and hired Ella Louise to come to the hotel. We also know that the next morning, Jarvis Alvarado gave his hotel bed sheets to his producer to throw them in the bins out the back."

He watched Anderson lean forwards, his expression changing to one of alert interest.

"But we also know Isabella Lennon spent the night with Jarvis Alvarado, and she doesn't seem to know anything about Ella Louise. So, I need to know what time the call was made to the escort agency and what time Ella Louise went to the hotel."

Anderson paused, as though deciding whether to

give up this information or not, and then spoke.

"They got the call at seven and she went straight over there. The body wasn't discovered until the next morning, but time of death would have been around ten or eleven."

Poole nodded. "Thanks." He turned to go and realised that Anderson was following him out of the door. He turned to look at him.

"Sharp's off having drinks with the chief. I'm coming with you."

"That's not how this works."

"Look," Anderson said, "I don't like you, but I want to solve this case and it looks like we're now working the same one. I need to be part of it."

Poole took a deep breath. "OK, but you can explain it to Brock."

They stepped out into the main office and headed for the canteen when Sanita called across to Poole from her desk. He changed his direction and moved towards her, cringing inwardly as Anderson did the same and came up alongside him.

"What is it, Constable?" he said, far more snappily than he would have if Anderson hadn't had been there. He cursed himself for being weak and influenced by his presence.

"We haven't found anywhere in Bexford that sells the brand of whiskey Jonny Turnbull had when he died. We're still looking farther afield, but I suddenly thought to check the hotel."

"The hotel? That's the first place we looked," Poole said. "They don't sell it."

"No, they don't, but they have it," Sanita said, smiling. "They don't have any behind the bar because it's some crazy expensive single malt that they only reserve for the special guests."

"Like Jonny Turnbull?" Anderson chimed in.

"Well, no," Sanita replied. "Apparently none of the staff gave Turnbull a bottle and neither did the manager or anyone else."

"Where was this stuff kept?"

"In a store cupboard out the back by the kitchens. It wasn't locked or anything, but you'd have to know where you were looking."

"So, Turnbull might have found his way back there on his own, or someone from the staff either showed him where it was, or got it for him and is lying?" Poole said.

"Looks like it, sir."

"Good work, Constable." Poole nodded before turning back towards the canteen.

"Sexy little thing, isn't she?" Anderson said quietly next to him.

"Shut it, Anderson," Poole hissed back, his fists balled at his side.

CHAPTER TWENTY-SIX

Poole glanced to his left at the inspector, who was squashed into the passenger seat as usual. His face was as hard and unreadable as granite, but there was a coolness emanating from him that made the hairs on the back of Poole's neck stand up.

The reason for this frosty atmosphere was clear: their new team member.

"You don't drive then, sir?" Anderson said from the back in an amused voice.

"No," Brock growled.

"Shame that. Must make it difficult getting around."

Brock emitted a low noise that could only be compared to a growl and Poole found himself accelerating harder in an effort to reach the hotel more quickly.

A few minutes later he swung the car into the now-familiar car park at the back, and the three of them stepped out.

"So are we going to ask Gina Glover if she called for the escort?" Poole asked as they began walking to the back entrance.

"We are," Brock grumbled. "That's if she's finished with her adoring crowd." He paused at the doorway. "Now listen, you two. We've got bugger all to go on here against any of them, and I find that in these situations it's best to just go in and do a lot of talking, accusing and riling, and see what sticks. So just go with it, OK?"

They nodded and followed him through the door.

When they reached the lobby it was clear that the party was over. It was empty apart from a middle-aged couple talking to the receptionist. Brock veered towards the bar area and stepped through the door.

Gina Glover, Mike Hart, Eli Patrick and Jane Marx were sitting around the same table the cast had gathered around previously.

"Inspector!" Gina said, her arms wide, one hand containing a gin and tonic. "Why don't you join us? We're having a little celebration!"

"I'm afraid, Miss Glover, that we're more

interested in a little celebration you might have helped with the other night."

"I'm sorry?" Gina said, her pale, freckled brow wrinkling.

"Did you make a call to an escort agency on Wednesday night and hire a woman named Ella Louise?"

Gina's expression changed slowly, as though her frown slid from her face to be replaced by a wide smile. She laughed, throwing her head back.

"You think I did what?! Honestly!" she said, shaking her head. "You are hilarious! Why on Earth would I do that? I mean, come on, Inspector, I'm not exactly desperate. I don't need to pay for it."

"Maybe you called her for someone else?"

Gina laughed again. "So now I'm some kind of high-class pimp?"

"We know she was in Jarvis' room that night, Gina."

The laughter vanished as quickly as it had come.

"You've seen the news, Gina. That girl died."

"What girl?" Gina said, putting her drink down on the table in front of her and sitting upright.

"Ella Louise, the escort that you called and hired. She was in Jarvis' room the night before he died, and now she's turned up dead as well." Brock folded his arms and stared at the group, all of whom were dumbstruck by the exchange.

"It wasn't Gina," a voice said quietly from the left of the group. They turned as one to look at Jane Marx, who was sitting with her head bowed, staring at the drink in her hands.

"Miss Marx, are you saying you called the escort agency?"

She nodded.

"What?" Eli Patrick said next to her. "Why on earth would you call an escort for Jarvis?"

"I'm sorry," Jane said, turning to him. "But Jarvis was very persuasive and he said he'd call off the whole launch if I didn't help him out."

"Help him out? What does that mean?!" Eli said, his cheeks reddening.

"Miss Marx," Brock said, stepping forwards. "I think it might be best if you came back to the station with us to give a statement."

Jane nodded, a tear rolling down one cheek.

"MISS MARX, just start from the beginning and tell us exactly what happened on Wednesday night."

Jane blew her nose and then looked up. Her eyes were red with tears as she glanced at Brock and Poole opposite her and then behind her to Anderson, who was standing in the corner.

She glanced at her newly appointed county lawyer, who was sitting next to her making notes but said nothing.

"Jarvis came to me that night and said he was bored in Bexford. He asked if I knew of anywhere he could find a party, something to do. 'Something exciting,' he said."

"And your first thought was to call an escort agency?"

"No!" she said suddenly. "Well, at least, not exactly." She slumped back down in her seat. "I knew Ella Louise from school; we both grew up in Bexford. We weren't friends or anything, but I met her a few weeks ago in town and we got chatting. She told me what she did and... well, I couldn't believe it." She shook her head again sadly and fresh tears sprayed the table. She pulled another tissue from the box that had been placed in front of her and dabbed at her eyes.

"But she seemed happy enough, and she definitely had money. It's funny," she said, looking past Poole's shoulder and staring at a point on the wall. "We'd been in a play together at school and she'd been a good actress. Better than Gina Glover, anyway." Her eyes focused again as she continued.

"Anyway, I remembered that I'd mentioned the *Foul Murder* launch to her and how excited she'd been. She said she'd always had a thing for Jarvis Alvarado. So, I called her." Her voice was hollow, as though the life had been sucked out of it. "If I'd known it would get her killed..." She looked down and sobbed heavily.

"Anderson," Brock said, "go and get Miss Marx some water, will you?"

Anderson glared at the inspector, but left the room anyway, returning a few moments later with water from the machine in the hall in a paper cup, which he placed in front of Jane.

"Thank you," she said in a weak voice before sipping at the cup tentatively.

"Please, Miss Marx, continue," Brock said soothingly.

She nodded again. "I called Ella Louise's agency —I didn't have her number—and said I had a job for her at the hotel. I thought I had to say it was a job or I'd get her in trouble, but I just thought she'd like to meet him and could maybe take him out or something. I thought Ella Louise would be a bit more his speed than me trying to show him around."

"And what happened when she arrived at the hotel?"

"I don't know. I let her in and showed her to

Jarvis' room and that was it. She was so excited," she said sadly, taking another sip of water.

"And what time was this?"

"About eight, I think?"

"And you didn't see Ella Louise again?"

"No," she answered, blowing her nose again.

"And what about Eli Patrick?"

The sudden change of direction made her look up. "Eli? What about him?"

"You and he seem close," Brock said.

"Eli is a very lovely man," she said, smiling through the tears.

"And was he part of this little arrangement?"

"No! He knew nothing about it!" she said defensively. "Eli didn't really get on with Jarvis or Jonny; he wasn't like them."

"And what were they like, Miss Marx?"

"I don't like to talk ill of the dead," she said quietly, "but they were selfish and rude."

"And when did you realise that Ella Louise had died?"

"Not until Friday," she said, her voice almost inaudible. "I saw it on the news."

Brock sighed and leaned back in his chair.

"OK, Miss Marx, that's all for now. Can I ask that you don't leave Bexford for the time being; we may need to speak to you again."

They watched as her lawyer escorted out of the room in silence. As the catch of the door clicked closed, Anderson advanced, leaning his hands on the desk.

"Alvarado must have killed Ella Louise," he said loudly.

"Why?" Brock asked thoughtfully.

"Because he bloody slept with her and it obviously went wrong, somehow. He killed her and then dumped her body."

"Isabella Lennon says she was with Jarvis from ten o'clock until the morning," Poole pointed out.

"She's lying," Anderson said, laughing as he got up. "She's covering up for him."

"Why would she cover up for a dead man?" Poole asked, getting annoyed now at Anderson trying to railroad the investigation towards a quick resolution.

"Who knows!" Anderson said, waving his hands in exasperation. "These actor types are all barmy!"

"And who killed Jonny Turnbull?"

Anderson paused and frowned for a moment. "Isabella Lennon must have done it."

"Why would she?" Poole asked, exasperatedly.

"Maybe Turnbull found out what Jarvis had done and Isabella wanted to keep it quiet."

"But why?" Poole said, almost shouting now.

"Why would Isabella want to cover up for Jarvis so badly?"

"She was mad about him!" Anderson shouted back. "You know what women can be like! She was probably obsessed with him or something!"

"God, you're a Neanderthal idiot," Poole said, putting his head in his hands.

"What did you call me?" Anderson puffed his barrel chest and advanced on the table.

"Anderson." Brock's voice cut through the room despite him only speaking quietly. "Go and inform Inspector Sharp of the latest developments. I expect he'll be back from his... meeting now."

Anderson glared at Poole as he answered with a snapped, "Yes, sir," and headed for the room.

"Come on, Poole," Brock said wearily. "It's been a long day. Let's go for a pint."

CHAPTER TWENTY-SEVEN

The familiar smell of stale beer hit Poole's nostrils as he and Brock entered The Mop & Bucket, its low ceilings and dim lighting making their eyes blink as they adjusted for the fading daylight outside, which entirely failed to penetrate the grimy windows.

"Two pints of Bexford Gold, please," Poole said as they reached the bar.

"Looks like we're not the only ones with this idea today," Brock said, nodding through the archway to their left where they could see a familiar, small group of people from Bexford Police Station. Sanita caught sight of Poole and waved. He waved back, his cheeks reddening as he turned back to the barman to pay.

"Bloody hell, Poole," Brock said, chuckling, "if

you're going to make it that obvious, you might as well ask her out for a drink."

"Sir?" Poole said as innocently as he could.

The inspector's open nature when it came to personal matters still tended to catch Poole off-guard, and seemed to go against his generally prickly nature.

"Oh, come on, Poole. I'm a detective, but you don't need to be one to see what's going on between you and Constable Sanders. Just don't leave it too late, that's my advice. Before you know it she'll be married to someone like Anderson and have three kids." Brock moved away from the bar and headed across to the table, leaving Poole in a state of shocked horror at the image of Anderson and Sanita in married bliss.

He snapped out of it and followed Brock.

Brock took a seat next to Davies and Poole tried not to flush again as Sanita pulled him a chair over from the next table.

"Thanks." He smiled at her. She smiled back at him and then turned to the table, where Roland Hale was talking.

"And so I told this bloke that I'd heard Jonny Turnbull was going to have a Viking funeral on the River Bex, and that they were just sorting the boat out now down at the park."

"And he believed you?" Davies said in awe.

"Of course he did; he worked for *The Sun*." The entire table laughed and descended into a series of smaller conversations and discussions.

"So," Sanita said, turning to Poole. "You wanted to have a talk?"

Poole's stomach lurched. What on Earth was he going to say? He hadn't really needed to have a talk with her, it had just sounded like that when he'd been trying to fill the awkward silence that always seemed to be hovering when they were alone.

The words of his conversation with Brock filtered through his mind and he found himself repeating them as though some hidden force were working his mouth.

"I was just wondering if you wanted to go for a drink sometime?"

The general hubbub from the table seemed to die down and he felt the hot prickle of eyes watching him. He swallowed, his gaze firmly locked on Sanita's brown eyes.

"I'd love to," she said, smiling. She turned to the rest of the table, who as one gave a small cheer amongst shouts of "about time", and "took them long enough".

Poole buried his head in his pint and grinned, his cheeks glowing.

POOLE STEPPED through the front door of his flat and stopped in his tracks, his mouth falling open.

"Oh Guy, you're here! Fantastic!" his mum said, jumping up from the sofa and hurrying over to him. She put her arm around him and guided him towards the six women who were sitting in his front room drinking white wine and eating chocolates from the various packets that were open on the table.

"Everyone, this is Guy."

"Hi, Guy," the women chorused.

"Er, hello," Guy managed, in shock at this invasion of his home.

"Now, Guy, you must meet Angela here," his mum said, guiding him around to a woman on the far side of the group who was the only person present who wasn't his mother's age.

She had bleached blonde hair, through which dark roots headed halfway down her head and sad, doleful eyes, which looked up at him through clogged lumps of mascara.

"Hi," Poole said, causing her to giggle and turn away.

"Angela is Debbie's daughter," his mother said, pointing to an identical, but older version of Angela to her right as though this was significant, like being the daughter of Queen Elizabeth the second.

"That's great, Mum, but I've had a long day. Can I have a quick word with you in the kitchen?"

His mum smiled apologetically at the group and followed him into the kitchen, which was a small offshoot from the main room.

"What the hell are all these people doing here?" Poole asked, opening the fridge and looking for something that was vaguely edible.

"I've joined a book club and it's my turn to host. Honestly, Guy, I did tell you."

Guy vaguely remembered her mentioning a book club, but it had been lost in the almost constant torrent of words his mother spilt on a daily basis.

He turned back to the fridge, holding a dubious-looking jar of pesto, his mum looking at him with concern.

"Guy, you really need to let go of all of this stress. Have you been using the oils I gave you for the bath?"

"Mum, the reason I can't let go of my stress is because she bloody lives with me!" he said grimly as he bent down to root in the cupboard for some pasta.

"Well, I can see that you are too stressed to know what you're saying at the moment, so I'll leave you alone. I think it's a shame you haven't got time to stay and be civil to young Angela though. She's a lovely girl."

Guy pulled the remaining pasta from the cupboard, leaned on the countertop and took a deep breath.

"Mum, I need my own space again. Bexford was supposed to be a fresh start for me, and here I am living with my mum, having book club meetings with people I don't know and scraping around for some dinner because no one's done any shopping again."

He looked up at his mum and saw her lips were pursed. "You know I've been looking for somewhere, but if you're that desperate to get rid of me, then I'll see if I can stay with a friend."

She spun on her heel and headed back to her group. Guy considered going after her but decided he needed to eat and sleep more urgently than appeasing his mother.

"SO, now we're going to have to buy a new dining table as well as a new lino?" Brock said angrily as he stared down at the gnawed table leg in front of him.

He was crouched in the kitchen of his home as Laura cooked a Mediterranean vegetable dish on the far side. The smell of chorizo wafting across to him was making him hungry, and being confronted with the latest damage report from owning Indy, he was struggling to stay rational.

"He's a puppy, Sam. What do you expect?"

"Well, I expect not have to replace everything in the bloody house," Brock said, getting to his feet. "Where the hell is the little vandal anyway?"

"Oh, I don't know, Sam. I'm trying to cook dinner. He was sleeping in the living room last time I saw him."

Brock trudged off to the living room to find Indy standing on the coffee table, eating a daffodil, which had once been carefully arranged in a vase that was now on its side, with water dripping onto the carpet.

Brock put the puppy on the floor, still chewing on the flower, and began wiping up the water while swearing under his breath.

"It's ready!" Laura called from the kitchen. He scooped Indy up and carried him through with him, a petal still hanging out of the dog's mouth.

"Oh, Sam, you shouldn't let him eat things like that; it might upset his stomach," she said as she laid the plates on the table.

Brock grunted and placed the dog on the floor before taking his seat.

After a few minutes of silent eating, Laura broke the silence. "So, what's wrong with you?"

Brock looked up from his plate in surprise, as though he had just remembered that she was there. "Nothing, sorry."

"It's this case, isn't it?" she said, reaching behind her and pulling a bottle of red wine from the wine rack. "It's all over the news. The press is going crazy over it all."

Brock sighed and shook his head. "There's just something wrong about it all and I can't put my finger on it."

"Then you need to look at it from a new angle."

Her matter-of-fact tone made him look up. He smiled at her. "You know I think the force could have done with someone like you."

She smiled back at him playfully. "Ah, come on, Sam. I wouldn't want to show you up now, would I?"

CHAPTER TWENTY-EIGHT

"He's destroying everything!" Brock moaned as Poole slowed the car as they came to a set of lights.

"Isn't that what puppies do though, sir? Chew things?"

"Well, yes, but that's why I've spent a load of money on all sort of toys. Soft toys, bouncy toys, squeaky toys. He doesn't touch them. He just goes straight for my bloody furniture."

Poole laughed and Brock turned to him.

"So where are you going to take Constable Sanders out, then?"

Pool stopped laughing.

"I'm not sure, sir."

"Well you better think fast; the whole station's

already talking about it. People want to know. You two are the new soap opera in town."

Poole felt his throat go dry at the thought of half the station talking about his potential romance with Sanita.

They swung into the car park of the Sinton Hotel and parked in an end bay. The square of sky visible to them from the courtyard was clear blue, but the morning was chilly, and their breath plumed about them as Poole locked the car.

"I want to go and look at the stage again," Brock said, heading towards the door to the back corridors of the theatre. When they reached it, they found it locked, and so turned and headed towards the hotel.

The lobby was quiet at this hour. Just a man in a suit relaxing in one of the leather armchairs, reading a paper, and the receptionist who was bent over her computer.

They walked straight through and out into the street, where the sun hit the golden sand-coloured stone that Bexford was almost entirely built from and gave the impression the place had been dipped in butter.

The large doors at the front of the theatre were firmly shut with no lights on inside.

"I'll call the manager," Poole said, pulling his phone from his pocket.

"He'll take a while to get here," Brock said, squinting as he looked down the street. "Why don't we sample the breakfast at the hotel while we wait?"

Poole's stomach rumbled in appreciation. "You read my mind."

BREAKFAST at the Sinton Hotel turned out to be an extravagant feast of toast, marmalades and jams followed by sausages, bacon, eggs, black pudding, mushrooms and beans.

Brock had devoured the lot between mumbling how he couldn't believe it was a "proper" breakfast and not "posh muck" that they had been served.

Poole watched as the food the inspector consumed directly correlated with his mood improving, and wondered if he suffered from low blood sugar.

They were drinking coffee and leaning back so their expanded stomachs could have room to digest when Terry Johnson entered the room and made his way towards them.

"Morning," he said, pulling gloves from his hands. "Can I ask why you want to get back into the theatre?"

"We want to look over the crime scene again," Brock said. "We thought there'd be someone there."

Terry laughed. "Oh, the theatre game's an evening thing, Inspector. We don't normally get in until around lunchtime, truth be told, though Jane sometimes comes in earlier to get things sorted. We're setting up for a new performance at the moment I'm afraid, so the stage is a bit of a mess. We had the first delivery of props for the play come in and it's piled there for the moment."

"Shouldn't be a problem," Brock said, draining the last of his coffee and rising. "Lead the way."

The three men headed back through the lobby onto the street before walking the short distance to the theatre.

"We'll take it from here," Brock said as they stepped inside. He headed off towards the doors on the far side, leaving Poole to give a hasty thank-you to the manager before joining him.

As they headed down the steps towards the stage, Poole had the same feeling he had the last time they had been in the vast space alone.

"This place gives me the creeps."

"What? A place where two people have been murdered in a week? You do surprise me," Brock said sarcastically.

Poole grinned. A well-fed Brock was a very different beast indeed.

The inspector paused next to him, turned, and looked back up the stairs they had just descended.

"This is where we found Jonny Turnbull," he said quietly. "How did they get him here?"

"Sir?"

"Jonny Turnbull was a young, fairly fit man. Someone got him here to kill him and I doubt they forced him physically or there'd be more evidence. They must have enticed him here somehow."

"Jonny was supposed to be a bit of a ladies' man, wasn't he? Maybe he snuck off with a woman?" Poole asked.

"Maybe. The man was a party animal by all accounts, so a good bottle of whiskey and the promise of more might have been all that was needed." He turned and looked back down to the stage.

Terry Johnson had been right: the stage was largely a mess. The entire far side was a mass of props and furniture, piled in an unorganised manner.

"Why were they both killed here, do you think?" Brock said as they continued downward.

"Empty space, easy to get to from the hotel I guess," Poole answered.

The inspector paused as they stepped out onto the

flat, carpeted area in front of the stage, which rose before them at chest height. "The door from the courtyard to in here was locked this morning. Why wasn't it locked on the night Jonny Turnbull was killed? He must have come in that way, because the cameras at the entrance to the car park and on the front door didn't pick him up."

"Someone from the theatre must have left it open," Poole said, jogging up the small flight of steps to the right which led onto the stage. Brock followed him and moved to the spot where Jarvis Alvarado had been killed.

Poole picked up an umbrella that was leaning against a sideboard and began tapping at the floor in various places.

"What are you doing?" Brock asked, staring at him.

"I was just wondering if there's a secret trapdoor or something we missed. You know, other than the one we saw when we were in the prop room with Jane Marx," Poole answered. He continued to tap until a cry from the inspector made him look up.

"Oh, bloody hell! You idiot, Sam!" the inspector roared.

He was staring upwards, his face contorted into a red rage.

"Sir?" Poole said, alarmed. He followed the inspector's gaze but could see nothing.

Brock ran towards the far side of the stage, his heavy tread thundering on the wooden boards as he did so. Poole took off after him and arrived as Brock stopped and pointed to the wall, his grey eyes ablaze.

"Get up that ladder, Poole," he said, in a tone that had Poole moving before he'd even asked what on earth this was about.

The ladder was a thin, metal affair that hung to the wall on tired-looking brackets. Poole put his foot on the bottom rung, pushed down on it in a half-hearted attempt to test whether it would hold his weight and began to climb.

He stared straight ahead at the crumbling brick that was now passing in front of him. He wasn't afraid of heights, but he wasn't a fan of them either. They tended to make him light-headed and wobbly, which was pretty much the last thing you wanted when you were at the top of a ladder.

After a few moments, a metal shelf appeared to his left as the ladder ran out. The shelf was roughly three feet wide with a foot-high barrier on either side made from thin metal poles.

Poole stepped up onto the last rung and leaned over onto the shelf, looking down its length.

"Well?" Brock shouted from below.

The sound made Poole look down and his vision instantly spun away from him. He clung tightly to the platform and closed his eyes until the motion in his head had stopped.

"It looks like an access gangway to the lighting rig," he called down. He heard a series of expletives from below before Brock replied.

"You can come down now, Poole, unless you fancy a trip along the gangway?"

"No!" Poole shouted. "I mean, no thank you, sir," he said, trying to calm his voice.

He slowly moved back to the ladder and descended with his eyes closed until his foot hit the floor suddenly, making him jump.

"Does it extend right out across the stage?" Brock asked. He was staring up into the black void above them and Poole looked too.

"Yes, it does," he answered. "Bloody hell, you can hardly see it at all from down here." The gangway hung in the gloom above the lights which shone brightly down towards the stage. There was no way it was visible unless you knew it was there and squinted sufficiently.

"I wouldn't have known it was there until you started banging on about there being another trapdoor," Brock said, moving back out into the middle of the stage.

"Sir?"

"It got me thinking about someone coming up to

kill Jarvis; then I realised what we hadn't thought of was something coming down to kill him." The inspector smiled. "Jane said we had to look at this from another angle."

Poole looked up. "You mean someone was up there when Jarvis was murdered? And they killed him somehow?"

"What was it that new pathologist said? That Jarvis was killed with a blow right on the top of his head? We first thought was that it had been someone tall, but then we thought of the sack, and sure enough, we found the weights in a sack in the prop room."

"Yes," Poole said, trying to follow what the inspector was getting at.

"It's all been about bloody acting, Poole," Brock said through gritted teeth. "Stupid, bloody acting."

They both turned as a noise rang out in the dark space beyond the stage. Poole saw the door that led to the corridors they had entered through previously bounce open slightly.

"Sir, I think someone was watching us!"

"Then come on!" Brock shouted, running for the steps that led down to the floor of the theatre. Poole ran straight for the edge instead, putting one hand on it to guide him as he jumped down. He landed and began running towards the door.

He reached it before Brock and burst through into the dim corridor beyond. He turned to his right and saw a figure in the distance running. He set off after them, his long legs eating up the distance.

He heard another door slam up ahead and powered on towards it.

He reached the door, which was still standing slightly ajar, and wrenched it open, stepping out into the bright light of the courtyard behind the hotel.

There was no one in sight, no sound other than the distant hum of traffic from the other side of the building.

He walked out into the middle of the space and turned slowly around, looking at the cars that surrounded him. No one.

Brock appeared through the door, his large face red—whether through exertion or anger, Poole wasn't sure.

"They vanished, sir," Poole said, shaking his head.

"We need to secure Gina Glover, Eli Patrick, and Mike Hart right now," Brock said, his chest heaving as he leaned on a silver Mercedes.

"Yes, sir," Poole said, moving towards the hotel door. As he reached it, Eli Patrick stepped out.

"Oh, morning, Sergeant," he said, a slightly confused smile on his face.

Poole grabbed him, spinning him around and putting his hands behind his back in one motion.

"Hey!" Eli shouted as Poole slipped cuffs over him.

"Eli Patrick, I am arresting you on suspicion of..."

"Oh, bloody hell, Poole, let him go!" Brock said, joining them. Poole looked at him in confusion.

"It's not him!" Brock cried, snatching the key from Poole and releasing Eli's cuffs.

"Did you see Jane Marx come through that door?" Brock asked Eli urgently.

"No," Eli said, frowning. "I was just looking for her. What's going on?"

"Poole," Brock said, ignoring Eli. "For goodness sake, get some backup here, will you?"

"Yes, sir," Poole said, pulling his mobile from his pocket.

CHAPTER TWENTY-NINE

"Gina Glover's not in her room, sir. No one seems to have seen her," Constable Sanders said as she approached from the staircase.

Brock swore under his breath. "Right, you stay with these two in the bar area." He pointed to Mike Hart and Eli Patrick. "No one leaves, OK?"

"Inspector, I insist you tell me what is going on!" Eli said, his plummy accent becoming even stronger in his anger.

"Sanders," Brock said, his eyes ablaze. "Take Mr Hart and I'll send Mr Patrick along shortly."

"Yes, sir," Sanita answered before ushering the producer away to the bar area.

"Mr Patrick, what is happening here is that I believe Jane Marx to have murdered three people, and may well have abducted a fourth."

Eli reeled backwards, the colour draining from his face as he desperately glanced at Poole, hoping this was some kind of joke.

"What? Jane?! But..."

"Did Miss Marx ever tell you of a place she had here or near here? A safe haven?"

"I... well, no, she didn't. She always talked about the theatre as her home, and this place of course."

"This place?"

"The hotel I mean. She's been working at the theatre for years, and has helped out here quite a bit, I think."

Brock spun to Poole. "Where's the manager of the hotel?"

"Michael Johnson? I don't know, I'll find him," Poole said, heading off towards the reception.

They had already rounded up his brother, Terry Johnson, and asked him if there were any places within the theatre that Jane Marx might hide away. He had said that there weren't other than the obvious ones. But they had already checked the prop room and the dressing rooms.

Now Gina Glover couldn't be found, they had to move quickly.

"I need to speak to the manager. Where is he?" Poole said to the mousy receptionist.

"He's in his office. Who shall I say is asking?"

Poole ignored her and stepped behind the counter, marching behind it until he reached the door on the far side, which he opened without knocking.

Michael Johnson was slumped over his desk, a dark pool of blood billowing from a wound on the front of his head.

"I need medical attention in here!" Poole shouted through the office door, thankful that they had called an ambulance at the same time they had called for backup. He moved across to the prone figure and took his pulse. He was still alive.

He swayed backwards as his head swam at the sight of the blood. He turned away and closed his eyes, taking a deep breath. His bloody father was bringing back things he wanted buried.

Two ambulance workers rushed in with the receptionist behind them, who screamed as she saw her boss on the table.

"Did Jane Marx come in here?" Poole asked her urgently, moving away from the body.

She stared at him, breathing heavily, and nodded.

He turned around, his eyes scanning everything in the small room apart from the body. The place was as tidy as an office ever was, and there was no sign of a struggle.

His eye landed on a wooden board on the wall

behind the desk. It was covered in rows of small, labelled hooks, each with a key hanging from it.

All except one.

He turned and ran out of the door and back along the rear of the reception desk as Brock approached.

“What is it?” the inspector said.

“It’s Michael Johnson. Jane Marx has whacked him over the head, but I know where she’s heading.”

CHAPTER THIRTY

"It's locked," Poole said, trying the handle of the door leading out onto the roof.

They had anticipated this and taken a second key from the maintenance man. Poole placed it in the lock and turned it slowly.

"Everyone get out onto the roof, but stay by the door and let me take the lead, OK?" Brock said, looking back at Constables Sanders and Davies, who were standing lower down on the stairs. He looked up at Poole.

"That means you too, you know."

"Yes, sir," Poole said, grinning.

Brock opened the door and stepped out into the bright sunlight.

The roof was constructed in the same golden stone that the rest of the hotel was made of and had a smooth, undulating nature to the large flagstones that covered it. Around the edge was a low wall of no more than three feet, and it was here that Gina Glover was sitting, mascara streaming down her pale cheeks, her hands bound with thick, plastic zip ties.

Jane Marx was standing in front of her, a long knife in her hand. The bright sunlight glinted from the blade as she turned at the noise of the door being opened behind her.

"Sshh!" she said angrily at them, before turning back to Gina. "Now, where were we?" she said, before shaking her hands out and taking a deep breath. "We recovered the DNA from the boot of your car," Jane said loudly. "There's no escaping it this time. You're going down." She bowed to her captive audience. "So, what did you think?" she squealed, running over to Gina and bending down in front of her.

Brock paused, aware that she could send Gina over the edge at any moment.

"It was... very good," Gina said in a quiet, teary voice.

"That was from series four, but I could do something more recent if you like?" Jane said.

"No, no," Gina said, trying to smile. "That was perfect."

"So, can I have the part?"

"Yes, yes, you can have the part. Shall we go downstairs and sort it out?"

Jane's eyes narrowed. She turned back to the inspector who had been slowly approaching and was now only ten feet or so from her.

"You're lying, aren't you?" she said to Gina, her eyes darting between her and the inspector. "You're just like the others—you say the right things but you never mean them!"

"I do mean them!" Gina said, her eyes darting to Brock's pleadingly. Jane's eyes followed hers. "You can be in the film, I'll make sure of it!"

Jane turned to her. "Do you think you deserve to be an actress, Gina?"

Gina stared back at her.

"Do you think you deserved your big break?" Jane walked to the other side of her and took a seat, lifting a lock of her bright red hair with the blade of the knife and studying it. "I've been waiting for my big break all my life, you know," Jane said quietly. "I was just a girl when I started working at the theatre. I thought if I could just be near it, just be part of it all, then I could learn. I could learn from real actors. Then eventually I would get a part. A small part at first, but I'd perform so well I'd be noticed. And then the world would really see." She smiled and stared up at the bright blue sky. "They'd all know my name then."

"Is that what Jarvis told you, Jane?" Brock said. "That he'd help make you a star?"

She looked at him with a blank stare.

"Jarvis? He wouldn't help me," she said bitterly. "He was only interested in one thing."

"Is that why you called your old school friend? To satisfy Jarvis' urges and maybe get in his good books, so he could put in a good word for you somewhere?"

"Everyone knew he had been given the role in the film," she said bitterly. "I just thought that if I could become friends with him, maybe he'd see my potential."

"And then what happened? Did Jarvis hurt Ella Louise, and you helped him cover it up?"

Jane's lip curled in amusement. "Is that what you think? That Jarvis killed her?" She laughed, a high and unsettling noise. "Jarvis was done with her in a few minutes. That's when I realised he was just like the rest of them. When I asked him if he would put in a good word for me, maybe get me an audition..." Her face turned dark. "He laughed at me. So, I decided to do something to make him listen."

"You killed Ella Louise," Brock said.

"Do you know she used to pick on me in school?

When I saw her again recently, she didn't even remember me at first. I had to tell her who I was, and then do you know what she did? She spoke to me like we were old friends. I couldn't stand her," Jane finished bitterly.

"And so you tried to blackmail Jarvis to get you a part?"

"He said he would get me onto the film, that he'd sort everything out. But he lied again. Why do you all lie?" she said, turning to Gina and placing her head on one side.

Gina said nothing, but recoiled from her.

"Do you know what that idiot told me next? He told me that he'd get me some work backstage. That I could be a runner on set. I said no!" Jane screamed suddenly. "I told him that I was an actress!" She looked down at the ground, and when she next spoke her voice was quiet with rage. "He laughed at me."

"So, you decided to get even. You dropped weights on him from the lighting gantry."

She frowned at Brock, a smile on her lips. "How did you know that? I didn't think anyone knew that," she said dreamily, as though remembering her actions. "It was really rather clever," she said with a faint smile on her lips. I used a rope that I ran along the lighting access gangway that had the weights all set up. It's funny, I didn't think it would actually kill him. I mean, I knew where he would be standing, we'd gone over it enough, but I still thought maybe I'd just hurt him. I knew no one would ever think to look up. Not with all those people who wouldn't have minded bumping him off sitting a few feet away."

"And afterwards?" Brock asked.

"Afterwards?" Jane asked him with a puzzled expression. "I just pulled the sack back up and tied it to a hook on the wall. I moved it into the prop chute the next day after your lot had left and then showed you," she said, smiling. "You believed me, didn't you?" She turned back to Gina. "You see, Gina? I fooled the clever Inspector Brock here! That's how good I am!"

"And why did Jonny Turnbull have to die?" Brock said, trying to keep the focus on him.

Jane laughed as she turned back to him. "Because he was in the way! I'd finally found someone who knew how I felt. Someone who deserved a break, just like me."

"Eli Patrick?" Brock asked. "Hasn't he already had his break? He's on the show."

"Oh, he deserves more than just being a side character on a TV show. He's going to the top, and I'm going to go with him."

"So, you thought getting Jonny out of the way would make Eli next in line for the role?"

Jane's eyes flashed angrily as she turned to Gina. "That was before I realised they were going to give the part to Gina here. So, Gina?" she said, leaning in towards her. "Do you deserve your big break? Have you thought of it every waking moment, dreamt of it? Tried everything you can do to be better, to be perfect?"

Gina said nothing, but stared back at Jane with a mixture of fear and repulsion.

Jane cocked her head to one side and then slapped Gina hard across the face. "Answer me, Gina!"

"I don't know!" Gina cried, her cheek glowing red where the hand had struck. "I don't know what you want me to say!"

"I guess it doesn't matter," Jane said lightly. "When you're gone, Eli will be in the lead role and he'll make sure I get my chance."

"I think you're looking for reasons why it hasn't worked out for you, Jane," Brock said, desperate to divert her attention. "But maybe you need to look at yourself."

"What would you know about it?" Jane hissed, turning to look at him.

"Only what I've seen of you. I just don't think you've got it, that star quality."

"Shut up! Shut up!" screamed Jane, her eyes bulging wildly as she waved the knife in front of her.

"Eli knows it," Brock continued, moving slowly towards her. "He knows you are never going to make it; he told me."

"Lies!" she screamed at him.

"It's not, Jane. He and I were having a good laugh about it earlier in the bar. The idea that you could actually be on TV!"

Jane screamed, a guttural, primal noise of anger, frustration and fury. She launched herself at Brock with a violent scream, the knife raised above her head.

Poole ran forwards, his heart pounding in his chest. He watched as Brock set his feet, ready for Jane to reach him. The whole scene seemed to play as in slow motion.

Jane Marx's arm swung down, the blade shining in the morning sun like a bolt of lightning.

Brock's thick arm swung sideways, hitting Jane Marx's at the wrist and sending it wide of its mark. She swung it back towards him and it sunk into his forearm as he moved to block it. He let out a grunt of pain as Poole arrived and hit Jane's waist with his shoulder. She flew backwards and landed heavily with Poole on top of her.

He looked into her eyes as her face turned into a wide smile. He frowned as he looked down and saw the knife vanishing into his gut in the middle of a growing circle of blood.

As his vision blurred, he saw a fist fly past his face and smash into Jane Marx's nose before the world swam sideways and he fell into the encroaching blackness.

CHAPTER THIRTY-ONE

Poole opened his eyes to see Sanita leaning over him.

"You're awake!" She clasped his face in her hands and kissed him on the lips, then pulled away suddenly.

"I'm sorry," she said, looking embarrassed.

"No, it's OK," Poole said. His voice sounded croaky and alien to his own ear. "Is the inspector OK?"

"He's fine," Sanita said, laughing. "He's been moaning about you diving in to save him, though. He says you never listen to orders."

Poole grinned, imagining Brock's annoyed grumbling, and knew what it really meant; that he'd been worried about Poole.

He looked up at Sanita, and suddenly the enormity of what had just happened passed through him like a shockwave.

"Did you just kiss me?" he said, wondering if he was dreaming.

"Yes," she said, smiling.

He smiled back at her. "If I'd known the rewards I'd have got myself stabbed before."

She laughed and punched him playfully in the arm when the door opened.

"So, you've decided to join us, have you?" Brock said, moving into the room and taking up at least a quarter of its space instantly.

"Hello, sir."

"Well, just don't think you've escaped any of the paperwork. I've saved it all for you."

"Oh, thanks," Poole said sarcastically. "That's what I get for saving your life, is it?"

"Saving my life?!" Brock said, his eyebrows raising so high they almost touched the ceiling. He turned to Sanita. "Is that what he's been trying to sweet-talk you with? Making out like he's some kind of hero? You were there; you saw what happened."

"And what did happen, exactly?" Poole said, trying to sit more upright and wincing in pain as he did so.

"I was just about to get the knife from her and

take her into custody when some idiot decided to jump on the sharp end of her knife. Luckily Constable Sanders here has a mean right hook and knocked Jane Marx out before you could skewer yourself any more."

Poole laughed and then moaned in pain.

"I think it's best he doesn't laugh, sir; he has got a hole in his stomach, after all." Sanita smiled at Poole. "Did you think you were still a constable and wearing a stab vest?"

Brock chuckled as the door opened again, and Laura Brock came in with a tray of coffees.

"You're awake!" she said with a large smile on her face. "Good job I got you a coffee as well!"

"It's not going to leak out of his belly, is it?" Brock said, taking the tray from her.

Laura rolled her eyes at him as she moved to Poole's side.

"Thank you," she said, kissing him on the cheek. "It was very brave of you to save Sam like that."

"Save me?!" Brock roared. "He's brainwashed the lot of you!"

Laura gave a conspiratorial grin to Poole. "I think we can have a lot of fun with this."

She pulled away and handed out the coffees from the tray while Brock held it.

"So where is Jane Marx now?" Poole asked once he'd managed to sit more upright and take a sip.

"She's at the station. I'm going to go and take a formal statement from her in a bit," Brock answered. Poole noticed he was drinking with his left hand, and for the first time noticed the bandage on the inspector's left forearm.

"Stitches?" he asked, nodding to it.

"Twelve," Brock answered. "But I think you beat me by ten or so," he said, smiling.

It occurred to Poole that he hadn't yet inspected his own wound. Suddenly the memory of the bullet wound he had sustained in the attack on his house all those years ago burned in his mind. The blood, the pain. Watching his friend die.

He tried to focus back on the case.

"I want to be there when you take her statement," he said firmly to Brock.

"I don't think that's a good idea," Laura said, frowning at him.

Poole's eyes remained fixed on Brock's, who was staring at him, as though trying to make his mind up.

"I need to be there," Poole said.

Brock nodded. "If the doctor clears you to go, then it's fine with me."

"Oh, Sam!" Laura said, shaking her head.

"Are you sure?" Sanita said next to him. She had

pulled away since the inspector had come into the room, but her hand now came to rest on Poole's arm.

"I'm fine," Poole said with a smile.

"The doctors said no important squishy bits were hit," Brock said. "So, I'm guessing you're all right to move about."

At the sound of his voice, Sanita pulled her hand away quickly.

"Well, all of this can at least wait until tomorrow, can't it?" Laura said. "You can take her statement tomorrow, can't you?"

Brock looked at his watch. "I guess so; it's gone midday already." He looked up at Poole. "That way you can stay in overnight, just to be sure."

Poole nodded. "Thanks."

"Come on, Sam," Laura said, tugging at Brock's sleeve. "Let's leave these two alone for a minute, shall we?"

One eyebrow rose on the inspector's face as he looked between Poole and Sanita.

"Oh, right. Fine," he said in an embarrassed tone. "See you tomorrow, Poole," he said before they shuffled out.

Poole turned to Sanita, who moved next to him.

"Thanks for punching Jane Marx for me." He smiled.

"My pleasure," Sanita said. She smiled back, but

the expression didn't last long. Her eyes seemed to grow in size, their bright whites shining against her light brown skin as they filled with tears. "You had me worried there, you know."

"I know," Poole said softly. "I'm sorry."

The door burst open as his mother flew in and threw her hands up in the air dramatically.

"Oh, Guy!" she wailed as she rushed to the side of his bed. "Are you OK?!"

"I'm fine, Mum," Poole said, knowing that this probably wasn't going to be enough to placate her.

She put her hands on his cheeks and kissed his forehead before pulling back and stroking his hair.

"I don't know what I would have done if..." She paused and looked up, seeing Sanita for the first time. "Oh, hello, love."

"Mum, this is Sanita," Poole said, flushed with embarrassment.

"Nice to meet you," Sanita said, extending a hand across Poole's chest.

Jenny Poole took it and shook it warmly. "Well, it's very nice to meet you, Sanita. You know, Guy never tells me anything about his work. Do you have a boyfriend?"

"Mum," Poole groaned, lying back on his pillow with his eyes closed.

"Not yet," Sanita said. "But I'm working on it."

Poole smiled.

LAURA BROCK CLOSED the door and watched Sam's large figure trudge down the corridor and into the kitchen.

She knew he had had a long day, and that his arm had hurt far more than he had let on. Still, there was something off about his manner when she had picked up from the station a few hours after their visit to Poole in the hospital. He had been quiet, withdrawn —distant.

Even when they had dropped by their friend's house to pick up Indy, he had waited in the car. She had made her excuses to their friends who had been looking after the pup and hurried back to the car, but Sam had taken the dog silently, stroking him morosely as she had driven them home.

She walked down the hall towards the kitchen where Sam was at the kitchen table, his back to her. She reached him and placed her hand on his shoulder as she moved round to look at him.

"Sam, is everything OK? It's just..." She stopped as she saw his face—ashen, grey, with large fat tears rolling down his cheeks. His large shoulders shook as Indy slept in his lap, oblivious.

Laura hugged him tightly, saying nothing.

Minutes later he finally spoke.

"The Cursed Detective, Laura. The cursed bloody detective."

CHAPTER THIRTY-TWO

"So, what about Jonny Turnbull?" Brock said. Jane sighed and leaned back.

They had already been talking for an hour again, going over Jane Marx's actions that had resulted in Jarvis Alvarado's death.

Now Brock was trying to fill in the blanks.

Poole had managed to make it, his stomach still heavily bandaged and hurting, but OK enough that he could move.

"Jonny was just like the rest of them. All he cared about was whatever he could get out of people."

"And you killed him so that Eli Patrick would be bumped up to the lead role in the film."

Jane smiled. "That was a bonus, but Jonny was a bigger problem than that." She leaned forwards. "Jonny had seen Ella Louise somehow, God knows where. At the hotel I guess. But he'd been threatening Jarvis with it to give him a part. I knew that it would only be a matter of time before he blurted something out. So, I decided to kill two birds with one stone." She shrugged and leaned backwards. "He was like an overgrown boy. All I had to do was show him that fancy bottle of whiskey and I got him interested. Then I just asked him if he'd ever had sex on the stage of a theatre before." She laughed at the memory. "He followed me like a puppy after that."

"And how did you kill him? He looked a strong young man to me."

She looked at Brock with an amused smile. "Inspector, don't tell me you think that a woman can't outmuscle a man?"

Brock said nothing, but stared back at her, stony-faced.

"He was no match for me, Inspector. I've studied Judo and there are holds you can put people in to that will snap a neck. He was drunk enough that he was laughing about it until he couldn't breathe anymore."

She looked past them, her eyes glazed. "If only they hadn't lied to me and had given me a part. Then we could have all been together in the film, like it should have been."

Poole looked at her vacant eyes and felt a wave of sadness.

This young, athletic, beautiful woman was going to spend the rest of her life in prison. And for what? A dream of becoming an actress, of becoming famous. Of walking those boards she had watched others tread for so many years while she stayed in the shadows and longed for her chance.

A waste of a life.

"ARE you sure you're OK to be here?" Laura said, looking at Poole doubtfully.

"I'm fine," Poole said, smiling.

The truth was his stomach was in agony. But, he reasoned, this was probably to be expected after being stabbed only thirty-six hours ago.

He certainly wasn't going to miss the ritual of visiting The Mop & Bucket once they'd closed a case, that was for sure. Even if it was going to give his mother another opportunity to grill Sanita about her marital status and who knew what else.

"And you?" Laura said to Brock in a quiet voice.

"Fine," the inspector replied with a dismissive grunt.

Poole got the impression there was something

more to this, but decided not to ask if everything was OK after seeing the look on Brock's face.

They stepped into the pub and were immediately greeted by Sanita, Davies, Roland and, surprisingly, Ronald Smith.

"Who invited Ron?" Poole asked Sanita out of the side of his mouth once he was at the bar waiting to order.

"Apparently the inspector did," she said, laughing as Poole's eyes widened.

"I know!" she said. "Who would have thought it, eh? I guess he felt sorry for him." Her expression changed and she looked at him strangely. "Are you sure you're OK?"

"I'm fine!" Poole said, exasperated. "I'm more likely to pop my stitches answering that every five minutes than I am coming to the pub for a victory pint."

"Fair enough," she said, laughing.

"Sanita!" Jenny Poole cried as she came up between them. "I was hoping you'd be here. I want to hear everything about you!"

Sanita smiled, but her eyes lingered on Poole and were full of fear.

"Mum, why don't you go and get us a table and we'll bring the drinks over?"

"Perfect!" his mum said and disappeared with

Laura Brock through the archway into the other room.

"Sorry about this," Poole said, giving Sanita an apologetic smile.

"Your mum seems lovely; I'm just not sure I want to face an interrogation before we've even been on a date."

"We're going on a date?" Poole asked, smiling.

"Well supposedly, but I've not been told where or when yet," she answered playfully.

Their drinks arrived as Poole's phone buzzed in his pocket. He pulled it out as he handed the money to the barman.

"Hello?"

"Guy? It's your dad."

He looked at Sanita, the smile fading from her face as she saw his expression.

"What do you want?" he said, turning away from Sanita.

"Remember what we talked about before? I have someone I'd like you to talk to."

"Who?"

"I'm outside with them now."

Poole's heart seemed to skip a beat in his chest. He spun around and stared at the small, grimy window to the right of the front door. He could see nothing through it.

The line went dead and he turned back to Sanita.

"Take the drinks over, would you? And can you tell Brock to come over here?"

She nodded, sensing that now wasn't the time to ask questions.

Poole turned back to the front door of the pub and stared at it as though it would reveal whether his father was standing behind it.

"What's wrong?" Brock said, his face full of concern.

"It's my dad. He's outside. Apparently, he has someone he wants me to meet."

Brock exhaled slowly through his wide nose and looked at the door. "We'd better go and say hello then."

CHAPTER THIRTY-THREE

As they stepped outside into the cool night air, Poole saw his father immediately. He was standing across the street with two other men. Poole noticed that they were standing at the middle point between two streetlights, maximising the shadows.

As he and Brock approached, he recognised the larger of the two men as the goon from outside the wine bar when he had last met his father. The smaller man to Jack Poole's right, he didn't recognise.

"Guy," his dad said with a sharp nod. The usual beaming smile he wore when they met was replaced by a hard, thoughtful look. "Inspector," he said, acknowledging Brock.

"What do you want?" Poole asked.

He watched as his father's eyes moved down to his stomach, which he realised he was holding protectively, his hand resting on the thick bandage below his shirt. He quickly moved his hand away and Jack's eye moved back to his.

"This is Stuart. He used to work for the Riverside gang."

Poole felt a jolt at the name—a name he hadn't heard spoken in almost fifteen years.

Poole turned to look at the man. He wore a small, thin goatee and had patchy, thinning hair on top of a small and angular head. He was standing with his arms folded and looked as though he was trying very hard to act casual. There was fear in his eyes, though, which darted between the gathered men, lingering slightly longer on Poole's.

"He wasn't part of what happened to us," Poole's dad continued. "But he knows what started it."

Poole felt his anger rising, but not with this man who was part of the gang that had shot him and killed his friend. His anger was with his father. *What happened to us?* Was that what he really thought? That this was something that had happened to him and not something he had caused?

Jack Poole turned to the man and gestured. "Go on," he said, his tone aggressive.

The man swallowed and looked back at the large man behind him. "The bosses knew someone was cutting in on their drug business, but we never had a clue who. We tried to put the word out, but they weren't using anyone we knew. People were coming into the area from outside."

"I don't care," Poole said suddenly, turning away.

"Guy!" Jack shouted, stopping him dead. "Please, just listen. Then you can go."

Poole turned around and waited. He noticed Brock hadn't moved next to him. He could feel the coiled tension of the inspector.

"Go on," Jack said to Stuart urgently.

"We used to hang out in this bar called Flakey's. Everyone knew it," Stuart continued, his speech rapid now, as though he wanted to get this over with.

"One day this woman came in and demanded to talk to the boss, bold as brass. We all had a good laugh at her, thought nothing of it, but she wouldn't leave. Eventually, she starts shouting that she doesn't want her husband to be any part of this drug business, and that she'd be willing to pay to get him out of it."

Poole moved his eyes from Stuart to his father, who was staring at him. Jack Poole's eyes were sparkling in the light, as though there were tears forming there.

"Then we got interested, hearing that this batty woman was willing to pay. We asked who this bloke's name was and she said, 'Jack Poole'."

The breath vanished from Poole in an instant as a roar of blood rushed in his ears. His hand instinctively went back to the wound at his stomach.

"We didn't have a clue who she was talking about, but we took a couple of grand from her and sent her on her way, promised to not involve him anymore. It was only later we realised that this must be who was cutting in on our business." Stuart stopped and turned to Jack Poole, whose eyes were still locked on his son.

"I didn't know I was part of anything, Guy," he said, his voice a hoarse croak. "I was just an idiot getting paid good money to not ask questions. I just handled the shipping. I never knew what was in it. Never wanted to. I only ever had stuff at the house that once, just once—while I was waiting for a new storage place to work out. Your mum looked in one of the boxes and found drugs. She thought she could get me out of it."

Poole staggered backwards, feeling as though his heart had been ripped from his chest and thrown on the floor. He felt Brock's hand land on his shoulder, steadying him.

"Don't blame her, son," Jack said stepping forwards, his arm rising slightly as though he wanted to reach out to Poole. "She was trying to help me, to help us both. But I need you to know what really happened so that we might have a chance of something."

There was no mistaking the tears now. They rolled down his father's face as his eyes pleaded with Poole's.

"I made bad choices, Guy. I put our family in danger. But I didn't know what I was involved with, how dangerous it was. And what happened that day was out of my control."

Poole turned and strode across the street, back towards the pub.

"Just talk to her, Guy!" Jack called out from behind him.

He opened the pub door and stepped inside, moving forwards until he could look through the archway and see the table where his friends were sitting. His mum was talking to Sanita and Laura, who were both laughing loudly.

"Poole," Brock said softly by his ear, his voice coming as a surprise to Poole, who hadn't seen him enter. "You don't know what that man said is true."

Poole said nothing but stared at his mother as he breathed heavily, a mixture of anger, sadness and blind panic welling in him.

"Not tonight, eh?" Brock said. "Have a drink, spend some time with your friends. You'll do no good talking about it in this state."

Poole nodded. He knew the inspector was right, but how could he go and sit down with his mother now without saying anything?

"Come on," Brock said, but instead of leading him through the archway to their friends, he led him to the bar. The inspector ordered three neat whiskeys and lined them up.

"Only one of these is for me," he said, knocking one back.

Poole downed the others in quick succession and leaned on the bar, taking deep breaths.

"OK." He nodded, standing up.

They walked through towards the table, and Sanita looked up at them.

"Where have you been? You should hear the stories your mum's told us about you growing up!"

Poole looked from Sanita to his mother, who was red-faced and beaming. She jerked a thumb towards Sanita and then raised it with an excited jiggle. He smiled at her weakly and took a seat.

Sanita gave him a curious look as Brock cut in.

"Right," he said loudly, clapping his hands. "Another case solved, and I'd like to propose a toast to the hero of the hour—someone who put their life on the line for a fellow officer." Brock turned towards Poole and Sanita. "And who has the meanest right hook in the whole of Addervale, Constable Sanita Sanders!"

There was a loud cheer followed by laughter as Sanita pulled a strongman pose.

Poole smiled, looked around the table and desperately tried to forget the scene outside.

He caught Brock's eye and the inspector gave him a nod of reassurance, as though telling him he was here for him.

Poole picked up his pint and drank deeply.

MORE FROM A.G. BARNETT

Brock & Poole Mysteries

An Occupied Grave

A Staged Death

When The Party Died

Murder in a Watched Room

The Mary Blake Mysteries

An Invitation to Murder

A Death at Dinner

For news on upcoming books and special offers, visit agbarnett.com

Read on to see the first chapter of the next in series!

WHEN THE PARTY DIED

"Do you think they'll remember to let him out after he's had his dinner?"

"Yes, Sam," Laura replied sighing.

"That's if they even remember to give him his dinner," Sam Brock grumbled.

"For goodness' sake!" Laura snapped. "He will be fine, he's four months old now, which in dog years makes him about twenty!"

"It would make him two, actually," Brock replied. "Anyway, you know what your parents are like. I went around to their house and found the front door wide open the other day, and they'd gone out!"

"We've done that, at least twice, as well Sam," Laura said. "Now can we try and at least pretend that you want to be coming out tonight?"

Brock felt a stab of guilt.

Tonight was the grand unveiling of a new exhibit at Bexford Museum. Which, along with this being its one-hundredth-anniversary year, had prompted a party. Which was why they now strolled through the centre of Bexford, in the glow of the afternoon summer sun. The yellow stone that the town was built from reflected the warm orange light around the streets, giving the place a surreal quality.

"So, tell me about this new totem pole then," Brock said looking down at the leaflet in his hand.

"You mean tell you again?" she said, giving him a look that could have melted steel. "Well, like I said to you the other day when you were so clearly listening to me, it's a mortuary pole."

"A mortuary pole? What on earth's that?"

"They were carved when someone important in the community died. Sometimes, like ours, they had the ashes of the person in a small door at the back."

"So it's like a giant wooden gravestone and grave, in one?"

"Yes, Sam," Laura sighed.

"Are you ok?" he said as they reached the path that led off the road and towards the museum.

"Yes, fine. Just got a lot on my mind, that's all."

"It's all going to be great," Brock said. "Try and enjoy yourself."

They climbed the shallow, well-worn steps that

led up to the arched doorway and were greeted by a young, pale woman with jet-black hair and eye makeup so dark it made Brock think of a panda.

"Hi Laura," the girl said, flashing a grin that contained a pierced upper lip.

"Hi Nancy, has anyone turned up yet?"

"Only Byron and Jemima," she said, grinning. "Don't worry, it's early!"

"I know, I know!" Laura said, taking the brochure that Nancy handed to her and passing it to Brock. "This is my husband Sam. Sam? This is Nancy."

Brock grunted a greeting at the young woman who returned the noise with a suspicious look.

"Oh, right," she said with barely disguised disdain.

Brock noticed that Laura was smiling as they moved through the hallway towards the main building.

"What was that about?" Brock asked. "She couldn't have been frostier if she'd been sitting in the freezer."

"Nancy's not a big fan of authority," Laura said still smirking. "She's got a lot of rebelling to get out of her system. She's a bright girl though, she wants to get into science."

Brock was about to ask at what time he could expect a glass of bubbly and some food when the sound of arguing echoed around the high stone walls.

"I'm well aware that this place doesn't run on hot air," a well-spoken female voice said in a sharp tone. "But what's the point in us being here if we're not trying to get the best pieces we can and display them?!"

They stepped into the enormous main room of the museum and saw a tall, slim figure standing in the middle of the main central aisle.

The room was bathed in the same golden light they had walked in outside. It filtered down through the glass roof whose frame was built from solid iron and covered with ornate mouldings of flowers and depictions of animals.

"We'll talk about this tomorrow," the woman said angrily. Pressing her thumb onto the screen of the phone to hang up and then staring at it as though it had personally offended her.

"Everything ok, Jemima?" Laura said as they approached.

"Oh, you're here!" Jemima said, turning. The annoyed expression on her face vanishing to be replaced by a broad smile.

The two women embraced, kissing air on either side of their cheeks as Brock waited in dread for his turn.

He had always hated the continental habit of kissing people on both cheeks. He found it even stranger when he was expected to kiss a woman on the cheek and then shake the hand of a man standing next to her. On the continent, of course, they kissed everyone. But the British weren't quite ready for that, and so had adopted this strange hybrid that left the inspector never quite knowing what he was supposed to do.

Jemima left him in no doubt though, grabbing him by his broad shoulders and air kissing loudly either side of his face.

"Nice to see you again," he said gruffly.

"So, is everything OK? Sounded like a bit of a heated conversation," Laura said, her face still concerned.

"Oh, yes," Jemima said. "Just the usual, you know, I think if Byron and I didn't argue at least once a day we'd both go mad!"

Laura laughed. "More like every hour for us," she said, linking her arm through Brock's and giving it a squeeze to let him know she was joking.

"Well, the catering team are all ready," Jemima said, looking over her shoulder. "I've left them filling the last of the serving trays and opening the champagne."

"Are the band here?" Laura asked.

"Yep, they've already sound-checked and are now sampling the canapés. We're all ready!" she said enthusiastically. "Now all we need is people to show up."

"Well, we've got half of my station coming so they should make up the numbers," Brock said.

"They'll definitely put a dent in the champagne at any rate," Laura said smiling. "So, is there nothing else to help with?"

"No, you've done enough all week. Why don't you go and show Sam the mortuary pole?"

"Will do, give me a shout if you need anything."

She pulled Brock along down the central avenue of the room where pathways set off left and right between rows of displays.

"Come on then," Brock said, hitching his suit trousers up. "Give me the lowdown on this pole's history and why it's such a big deal."

"Well, mortuary poles are the rarest kind of totem pole. Like I said before, they were basically a kind of tomb with a recess that the body or ashes could be buried in."

"And does yours have a body in it?"

"Sadly, no,"

He looked at her, his eyebrows raised.

"I just mean it would be a better find for the museum that's all, but there was nothing in ours."

"Where did you find it again? Some manor house wasn't it?"

"Otworth Manor. It was in one of the barns on the estate, been there decades apparently. The Pentonvilles have lived at the manor for centuries and some ancestor of theirs brought it back from Canada at some point. We're still looking into it. Anyway, William Pentonville died a few months ago and this piece came to the museum."

"Well it's bloody impressive," Brock said as they reached the base of the wooden pole. The main trunk of it was carved into two large figures, each with a smaller figure on its lap. A second carved trunk ran across the top of the pole to form a "T" shape, it too was ornately carved, but this time with a single figure.

It was roughly fifty feet high, reaching up to the second floor of the building, which consisted of a balcony that ran around the entire room.

"So, this Pentonville chap just left the totem pole to the museum?" Brock asked.

"I think so, yes. Why?" Laura said, recognising the glint in Brock's eye.

"Just odd, isn't it? I mean why this thing in particular? Especially if it had just been stuffed in some barn for years. There must have been other stuff there that the museum could have benefitted from, not just this."

"Can you just turn yourself off for one moment? Not everything needs an investigation."

"Sorry," Brock said, somewhat surprised by her reaction. He pulled her towards him. "I'm proud of you, you know? This stuff is amazing."

"Sam," she said softly, looking down at her own shuffling feet.

"What is it?" he asked, suddenly concerned. Laura was never nervous like this. She was the one who always had everything together.

"Just wait here a minute," she said suddenly, turning and heading back the way they had come.

Brock stared after her. She had been in a strange mood all day and for some reason, she was putting him on edge.

He turned slowly and looked back up at the totem. The thing was somehow beautiful and ugly at the same time.

He heard voices echoing in the large room behind him and turned to see the group from the station approaching. They were an odd bunch, seen from a distance.

Daniel Davies was on the left; a tall gangly lad who he was fairly sure had an ancestor who was a pencil. Next was Roland Hale, an overweight, small-eyed man who had a sense of humour that centred around irritating other people. Then there was Sanita Sanders and Guy Poole. He noticed how closely they walked to each other, their arms in danger of brushing together at every step. Ah, young love, he thought.

"Hello, sir," Poole said as they arrived. "We're a bit early, but we were told you were down here."

"Is this it?" Roland said looking up at the totem behind them.

"It is," Brock said turning and looking at it. "What do you think?"

"I think it's blooming ugly," Roland replied. "What's the point of it?"

"You bury someone important in it apparently."

"Blimey," Roland said. "Just set me on fire and go and have a pint. Don't bother carving anything."

"Thanks," Poole said. "Duly noted." He turned to Brock. "Where's Laura?"

"Nipped to the loo I think." Brock's eyes twinkled in the dim light of the museum. "Shall we sneak up to the next floor and have a look at where the body goes?"

There was a chorus of approval and the group moved towards the lift. They squeezed into it, with Roland taking up more than his fair share. They arrived at the mezzanine level with its bizarre arrangement of weapons, voodoo dolls and shrunken heads.

The local kids liked to spread rumours that they were specifically those of school children, shrunk by a former deranged teacher of the local school. The truth was they were long forgotten tribesman from South America, but the stories were somehow more fun.

They moved around until they were level with the top of the pole's cross piece and stared at it. It was right up against the gangway and Poole ran his hand over the smooth surface of the wood.

"Not much from the back is it?" Davies said.

He was right. The back of the pole was a flat plane of wood with no sign of the decoration on the other side.

"I guess people aren't meant to look at this side," Poole said. "Is that where the body was kept?" he said, pointing towards a crack in the horizontal section of the pole which formed a perfect rectangle.

"Looks like it," Brock said leaning over. He frowned as his eyes focussed on the upper line of the panel. "Someone hasn't been very careful with it," he said standing up. "Look at those chips in the wood."

Poole leaned over with the others.

"Looks like someone's used a crowbar on it,"

Sanita said. "Was there anything in it when they opened it?"

"No," Brock answered thoughtfully. Something was coming back to him from when Laura had been talking about this piece a few days ago. "I'm not sure it was the museum who opened this though," he said running his large hands over the fresh marks in the wood.

"What do you mean opened it?" Laura asked from behind the group. She was heading from the elevator with a frown.

Brock turned to her. "Laura, did you say that the museum never opened this panel?"

"Of course not, we didn't want to damage it. When we went to see it at the Manor we took ultrasound equipment to check there was nothing in there. Why?"

She moved past him to the edge of the railing and looked across at the pole, her hand reaching out immediately to the cuts in the wood. When she turned back to them, her face was pale. "Sam, we never opened that panel, and it wasn't like that when we looked at it at the manor. There were no chunks out of it like this."

"When was that?"

"On Wednesday."

Brock nodded and turned back to the pole. He

reached out and knocked on the wood. The sound came back with a dull noise. He continued knocking, moving his hand along the wood until the noise changed and became lighter. He turned to Laura as he moved his hand back and knocked where the sound became muffled.

"There's something in there."

"There can't be!" Laura said shaking her head.

"Those marks show that someone tried to open this," Brock said pointing to them. "You said the ultrasound showed it was empty, so if it's not empty now, then whoever tried to open this must have succeeded and put something in it."

"But why would—" Laura began and then stopped, turning to her husband.

Brock took a deep breath and turned to the rest of the group. "Poole, Sanders, stay here and make sure no one comes near this thing. Davies, Hale, get down to the bottom and make sure no one comes up in the lift or the stairs."

He watched the two young officers nod back at him. "Well, go on then!" he prompted. They jumped into action, as though someone had jerked them on a piece of string. Davies heading off with his gangly, awkward gait and Hale next to him with his tubby waddle.

"We need to get this panel open," Brock said

turning back to Laura who was still standing in shocked silence.

"Where's your caretaker chap? Frazer isn't it?""

"Yes," she nodded, her brow furrowed. "He'll be in the basement, I'll come with you."

They headed towards the lift and stepped inside in silence. Brock half turned to her and she folded her arms, staring resolutely ahead.

"Is everything ok?" he asked.

She sighed. "No Sam, everything is not ok. Someone's chipped our new bloody exhibit and hidden God-knows-what inside it."

"Well, yes," Brock said, turning to her. "But you just seem, I don't know. Like there's something else going on."

She snapped to him and he saw tears in her eyes. "Yes, there's something else going on!" she screamed at him as she rooted around in her handbag. Brock stared at the brown leather accessory with suspicion. Laura's wretched bag had always held a certain amount of fear over him. When on the odd occasion she asked him to find something in it, it was all he could do to not come out in cold sweats. The thing was a labyrinth of bits and bobs and you could be stuck there for hours looking for the desired object.

She pulled her hand out and held up what

looked at first like a pen. He frowned and peered closer as the lift pinged and the doors began to open.

"Is that—?" he said, his eyes widening. He took the object from her and stared at the small digital screen on one side. It had a line running down the right-hand side and a much fainter one to the left. He looked to the key which was printed next to the display and stared at it. A single line meant you weren't pregnant, two lines meant you were. "Does this mean that—?" he said looking at Laura as the lift doors closed again.

"I don't know!' she said rolling her eyes. "Look at the bloody thing! I mean, is that two lines or not?!"

Brock stared at the screen again. The line on the left was so faint, it almost wasn't there when you stared directly at it. "I don't know," he shrugged. "So you're? —"

"Just a few days late, it could be nothing." She took the test from him, threw it in her handbag and wiped her eyes. "Come on, let's go and find out what's going on with this pole."

He watched her storm out of the lift in a daze before shaking his head and following her. He passed Roland Hale and David Davies who were both standing by the foot of the totem pole and staring up at it.

"I'll be honest," Brock said as he caught up with

his wife. "Leaving those two at the bottom of the thing means we could well come back to it burnt to the ground."

"It's this way," Laura said, turning left down one of the rows of displays and clearly not buying his attempt at lightening the mood.

"We'll get another test, then we'll know," he said.

"Yes, and then we'll know," she replied, the resignation in her voice telling him that she had already made her mind up about what the answer was going to be. "But for now, shall we try and find out why someone's put something into my exhibit?"

Brock said nothing but followed her down the aisle, his mind in a whirl.

Was this it? Were they finally going to be parents? His mind moved away from the growing excitement he could feel in his gut to darker thoughts. Here they were at what should have been a moment of excitement and instead were set on this grim errand. And it was grim, he was sure of that. No one goes to the trouble of cracking open an artefact like that and putting something inside it without the reason being very troubling.

Laura opened a heavy door in the wall and they stepped through into a cool, dark corridor. They turned left and descended a steep staircase lit by fluorescent strip lights.

"The guy actually works down here?" Brock said, trying to think of something to say in the circumstances.

"Yes, Sam," Laura's tone was curt.

"I know you've told me that before, I just never thought it would be so, well, grim."

"Don't say that in front of Frazer, he's likely to smack you one."

Brock pictured Frazer as they descended into another short corridor. He had only met him a few times, and always out of the context of the museum. Usually at some staff do, Christmas dinner or summer barbecue. The white-haired, softly spoken Scotsman didn't seem the type to throw punches, but Laura had sounded as though she'd meant it.

He wasn't sure why, but Brock had always disliked the man. There was something about the eyes that set his teeth on edge.

Laura knocked on a door set into the wall on their left.

"Come in," a voice came from the room beyond.

Laura opened it and stepped through with Brock following her.

"Frazer? We need your help."

Frazer was standing facing them, his hands leaning on a small table either side of the laptop in front of him. He was a spritely, impish face man in his sixties. Thin-rimmed spectacles rested over warm, sparkling blue eyes. A wild mop of white hair contrasted with his neat beard.

"What's wrong?" he said standing up.

"We think there's something—" she paused and looked at Brock.

"We think there might be something in the totem pole," Brock took over. "We need to open it now. Have you got anything to pry it open, like a crowbar?"

"Aye, I have," Frazer said moving around the desk. "And I'm glad to see you here Sam, I've just noticed that someone tried to break in here last night."

"Break in?" Laura said. "Where? How?"

"I'll show you, it's where the crowbar is anyway."

The followed him back into the corridor and along until he opened a door on the left wall. They entered a large room which extended into the distance along rows of metal shelving which reached up to the ceiling.

"So, this is the storeroom?" Brock said looking around.

"Are you trying to impress me with your detective skills Sam?" Frazer said chuckling.

Laura laughed as well, apparently breaking her

previous bad mood. For some reason, this annoyed Brock more than he had wanted it to.

On the far side of the room, they came to a double-doored fire escape that had a length of thick chain slung around its push-open bars.

"That doesn't look very safe for a fire escape," Brock grunted.

"I've just put it on now while I can sort the doors out," Frazer said as he bent down and unlocked the padlock securing them. "Someone tried to force the mechanism." He pushed the doors open and stepped out into an alleyway which ran along the back of the museum. Look for yourself," he said, gesturing to the doors.

Brock and Laura moved closer and looked.

"Someone's tried to lever it open alright," Brock said peering at it. He got up and looked up and down the alley. One ended in a high stone wall, the other led back out to a side street. "You've got a security camera?" Brock said pointing to a light-grey shape on the wall as it ended at the street.

"Aye, just one that points to the entrance to the street, but someone smashed it with a rock or something last night. I was just trying to look at the footage when you came in but there's nothing there."

"You've got an alarm system presumably?"

"It didn't go off. It's all triggered by motion sensors inside, so if they didn't get in?" He shrugged.

Brock nodded and then fell silent. He stared at the door thoughtfully for a few moments, before he jumped back into life.

"I need you to stay here a moment until I can get an officer down to secure the scene," he said.

"Will do. I was due a cigarette break anyway," Frazer answered, winking at Laura.

"Where's this crowbar?" Brock snapped.

"It's back the way we came, to the left of the door back into the hall. I use it to open crates down here sometimes."

Brock grunted and turned back into the storeroom.

"What time does he normally arrive?" Brock asked as Laura caught up with him moving back down the metal aisle.

"Who, Frazer? I've no idea. He seems to practically live here, to be honest. Why?"

"I'm just wondering how long it took him to notice that someone had tried to break in. I mean, it's six o'clock in the evening."

"Well, how was he supposed to know if the alarm didn't go off? This isn't the Natural History Museum in London you know. We're not exactly hi-tech."

Brock said nothing and continued with his long

stride, Laura hurrying to keep up beside him. They reached the door and he walked the wall to the left until he found the crowbar and they made their way back into the museum.

The large room was a different place than the one they had left. Suddenly the high glass panes above them reflected voices and the sound of glasses clinking.

Brock looked down at Laura beside him and saw the lines of concern etched on her face. What was she thinking about right now? Tonight's party? What was in that totem pole? Or whether their dream had become a reality and she was pregnant?

As they reached the main avenue between the exhibits they glanced back towards the entrance. Waiting staff were milling around and setting out the glasses and bubbly on white-clothed tables.

"The plan is to keep everyone up there for a while with the drinks and nibbles, then move everyone down to the pole at around seven," Laura said, guessing what Brock was thinking.

They turned back towards the pole where Hale and Davies were still standing. Hale was looking in through the glass of a display case, Davies standing to attention at the base of the pole. His head swivelled left and right periodically looking for people to turn away from the area.

Brock said nothing to them as they passed, but headed straight for the lift where they rose in silence until the doors pinged open and they made their way to Poole and Sanita.

"Here we go then," Brock said as he hefted the crowbar. "You might want to stand back a bit," he said to the group. Laura scowled at him but moved back anyway.

He teased the prongs of the bar into the gap at the top of the panel where the wood had already been damaged and pulled downwards. There was a creak of wood as the panel gave way and fell out in front of them.

There, squashed into the recess of the mortuary pole was a man. His lifeless eyes stared out at them, unseeing.

Printed in Poland
by Amazon Fulfillment
Poland Sp. z o.o., Wrocław